T0128951

Eyes of the Owl

ALSO BY SHERRY WILLIAMS

Tales of Turtle River

Eyes *of the* Owl

SHERRY WILLIAMS

EYES OF THE OWL

This is a work of fiction. All of the characters, names, incidents, organizations, and dialogue
in this novel are either the products of the author's imagination or are used fictitiously.

iUniverse books may be ordered through booksellers or by contacting:

iUniverse
1663 Liberty Drive
Bloomington, IN 47403
www.iuniverse.com
1-800-Authors (1-800-288-4677)

Because of the dynamic nature of the Internet, any web addresses or links contained in
this book may have changed since publication and may no longer be valid. The views
expressed in this work are solely those of the author and do not necessarily reflect the
views of the publisher, and the publisher hereby disclaims any responsibility for them.

Any people depicted in stock imagery provided by Thinkstock are models,
and such images are being used for illustrative purposes only.
Certain stock imagery © Thinkstock.

ISBN: 978-1-4917-9672-6 (sc)
ISBN: 978-1-4917-9673-3 (e)

Library of Congress Control Number: 2016907231

Print information available on the last page.

iUniverse rev. date: 05/12/2016

ACKNOWLEDGEMENTS

To my husband for illustrating the front cover and title page

To Mary Kay McAlister for her valuable support as a reader and editor

To Xan Griswold for her many hours of edititing

And to my writing group, without whom I would be at a loss

Turtle River, Florida

September, 1995

Caleb was drawing owls again. Twisted, leafy tree branches, with three owls— one so deep in the shadows, only its eyes showed through. It's all he ever drew. Sometimes the owls were flying in and out of shadows and light— so realistic, yet dreamlike. Surreal, Ms. Coplan, our eighth grade art teacher, called it.

Then there was *my* pathetic piece of work. Why couldn't I get my drawing to look like what I remembered? Me, Missy Vicelli, riding Rain bareback, clinging to her silver mane, flying across the Pennsylvania hills. I could even remember her earthy smell. I wondered. Why? Why did we have to sell our farm and move back to Florida? Why did I have to start eighth grade at a school where I had no friends? If Mom hadn't left us, we'd still be in Pennsylvania.

Loud sounds of hysterics invaded my thoughts. Of course. It was Amber Ramos, one of the two snooty cheerleaders that I was unlucky enough to have sitting beside me.

"Come on Latanya, you didn't tell him that!" she said.

"I sure did," said Latanya Hastings, the other one.

Latanya was trying to braid Amber's silky red hair to look like her own African American hair. Hers looked like it had a zillion braids.

"Girls, get some paper and start working," said the substitute teacher we had because Ms. Coplan's daughter was sick.

Latanya popped her gum. "Yeah, we will," she said. But when the sub walked away, Latanya was still at Amber's back. They were

1

yammering and laughing about boys they'd been out with—bragging for everyone in the room to hear. No-brain doll babes. That's what I called them.

"You know, it would be so cool to be a make-over artist," said Latanya.

Amber turned her green, cat-like eyes on me. "After you braid my hair, why don't you practice on Missy," she said.

I felt a prickling on the back of my neck. They're going say something about my ears, I thought.

Latanya looked at me. "You know, you would look better if you'd have somebody style your hair. Pale complexion with blond hair and brown eyes is good, but your *hair. . .*" She clenched her teeth. "I don't want to sound mean, but you do need to do something with it. Give it some body. I can fix it for you."

I gave her a lame smile and shrugged my shoulders. I thought, *they're crazy if they think I'm going to jump up and down because they want to make me over.*

"She is cute in a way," said Amber. "But people think she's a boy."

"Amber!" said Latanya.

"No, really," Amber went on like I wasn't there. "She's so flat in the front and then she's always in those jeans and t—"

"Why don't ya'll, shut up!" cut in a male voice from across the table. Caleb Jones was smiling, his deer-like eyes looking at me. "Don't listen to them, Missy, they're just stupid." His eyes shifted back to his drawing.

By that time my face felt like a hot coal.

"What's going on over here?" The sub was standing over Caleb. Then she saw his drawing. "That's beautiful! She said. "Where do you get your ideas?"

Caleb smiled again. Deep dimples in his cheeks. His skin a deep African brown. He pointed to his head. "Right here."

That may have seemed like a conceited thing to say, but I didn't think Caleb was at all conceited.

Latanya leaned across the table toward him and looked at him with her enormous brown eyes. She fluttered her long curly lashes. "Hey Bro, when you going to give me one of your pictures for my room?"

"Got one for you at my place. I'll bring it tomorrow," he said.

"Where's your work?" The sub looked at Latanya and Amber.

"We finished ours. We took 'em home," said Amber.

Mrs. Funk didn't buy it, and told them both they'd get a zero for the day if they didn't get busy. It was about time. But Latanya didn't move from behind Amber, and the sub went to her desk which was opposite our table, sighed, and picked up a yellow pad. *I wish they'd get in trouble*, I thought.

I needed a picture of Rain. I didn't know how Caleb did it, but I needed something to look at if I was going to draw it. Trouble was, half our stuff was still in boxes, and I had no idea where my pictures were. Anyhow, my mind was a wasteland, ever since we'd come to Turtle River. I missed my best friend, Ann Marie, and wished she'd hurry and write. I'd written twice. If her parents weren't still in the Dark Ages, she'd have a computer and we could have e-mailed.

What was that sickening smell in the air? Oh, it was Amber's perfume she'd sprayed all over her neck and arms. Latanya was still behind her making thin russet ropes out of her hair. And that sub was just going to let them get away with it. *Figures. Those kind of girls always get away with things.*

Caleb was engrossed in his work. *Why does he always draw owls?* There was something about him that was different from all the others. He was nice to everyone for one thing, and even though a lot of girls thought he was hot, he didn't seem to notice. I liked how he looked. His nose straight and flaring at the nostrils. With his hair cut close—

Oh God! He's looking, he caught me staring.

"Say, you goin' on that field trip Monday with ecology class?" he asked.

I nodded. "Yeah, sure." I wondered why he cared. But before either of us could say more, someone burst into the room, loudly rapping and jerking to a beat.

It was Caleb's brother, baggy pants, earrings and dreadlocks.

"Joshua Jones here, Teach!" he said slapping her desk as if it were a drum.

"Joshua Jones, do you have a late note?"

"No ma'am, don't need one. Was helping the shop teacher."

"Well," she said, "I think you do need one, or I'll give you a detention slip for tardiness."

3

"Aw, I can't get no note. He ain't there no more." Joshua grabbed the staple gun from the desk and shot a staple into the air.

"Put that down!" shouted the sub. She jumped up and grabbed it.

"I always help him after class! You can ask anyone." Joshua faced the class with his palms up and mouth open.

"He does help him," said Latanya.

The sub took her yellow pad and scribbled something.

"What's that you're writing?" he asked and tried to grab the pad.

"Sit down! Before I really write you up!"

"Okay, okay," he said and started to meander toward my table.

Joshua and Caleb were both in the eighth grade, but Joshua was smaller and younger than Caleb. I figured Caleb must have been held back a year, but he was definitely more mature and smarter. Caleb was quiet, Joshua was loud and hopped around like a little toad.

"Hey Latanya," he said, and ran his fingers across her backside.

"Chill, boy!" she said.

I watched him pull a chair to the end of the table next to Latanya and Amber. I looked at Caleb, then down at his drawing. The eyes of a large owl looked back at me, and for one weird moment I felt a connection with it, then in an instant the feeling was gone.

CHAPTER 2

Home

Just inside the front door of my house was a small entry with the hallway to the great room straight ahead. A little to the right of the entry were the stairs to the second floor where Dad's bedroom was located. To the left of the entry was a passage way that led to my bedroom, the bathroom and the boys' bedroom. I had a bay window and window seat in my room, from where I could look out over our front driveway to the pine woods across the street—spindly pine trees, different from the mammoth ones in the north. And instead of grey sky and green mountains, I saw puffy cumulus clouds set in a cerulean blue sky.

I curled up in my window seat with a letter from Ann Marie.

> ... new house sounds terrific... met a lot of new kids. Jen Bradley and I went to a hay ride party last week. What a blast!

What is this, Ann Marie? Jen Bradley? We used to laugh about her and call her snooty.

> Remember Matt Conners? He used to ride our bus, and he's a year ahead of us. He's really changed in the past year. Jen says he likes me, and he's planning to ask me out!

He's not the only one who's changed, Ann Marie!

. . . I still ride Billy Boy when I find time. I saw Rain last week. Mr. Ebner is taking good care of her.

Thanks for reminding me that Rain will never be mine again?

Bye for now. Write soon.
Love, Ann Marie

Amazing what a month could do. I tore the letter into pieces and tossed them at the waste basket. I don't need turncoat friends. But then, what did I expect? I was gone—she'd moved on with her life.

Tears stung my eyes. I stared out the window, like a bird wanting to fly free from a cage, yet at the same time wanting to stay where it's safe and secure. For an instant Caleb Jones popped into my mind. But then I saw my little brothers across the street. They were running from the woods, fishing poles in hand, with Sam, our black Lab, running ahead of them. I went out the front door and they came up the porch steps wide-eyed, gasping for air, their blond hair sticky with sweat. Sam barked nonstop.

"What's wrong? Quiet, Sam!" I stomped my foot and clapped my hands at him, and surprise—he actually stopped barking.

Both boys were talking at once.

"Slow down," I said and looked at Richie "What is it?"

"A dead cat!" Ryan burst out.

"Shot full of holes," said Richie "All bloody an' hangin' from a tree!"

I got a sick feeling, then got angry. How could anybody do something like that? That could have been Sam. Or what if the boys had come on the scene too soon and caught the creep with the gun?

"You guys better stay away from those woods," I said. "And Sam isn't supposed to run loose like that."

The boys looked up at me like scared little birds.

"We didn't go near *his* house," said Richie. We just wanted to get to the river."

His house was the Weavers' mansion, a fortress at the end of our street, hidden by trees and set on the river. The son, Doyle Weaver was about my age. He scared the boys and told them to stay out of *his* woods the first time they passed near his house on their way to the river to fish. I had told them to keep a good distance away from the Weaver's property after that.

There was always something weird about Doyle. I first saw him on the day we moved into our house. Sam got loose and ran into the woods, and when I caught up, Doyle just appeared out of nowhere. He came up and smiled. It was an evil smile, and his icy blue eyes first fixed on mine, then moved to my torso. Really creepy. I clicked Sam's leash onto his collar and ran, pulling Sam through the woods until we got near home when he ran ahead of me. The next time I saw Doyle was in Ecology class, and that's when I learned his name.

"Do you think *he* did it?" asked Richy.

"I don't know. Put Sam in the back yard and wash him off. He's all dirty. And get yourself cleaned up for supper. Nana's ordering pizza."

"Don't be so bossy," said Richie, but he grabbed Sam and headed around back.

Ryan lingered and gave me a tight hug around the waist. "Poor kitty."

I pushed him toward the bathroom. "Wash your hands," I said, "and change your shirt and pants. Nana will be calling any minute."

I had to take care of Ryan, five, and Richie, seven, a lot the past two years. Having Nana and Pop Pop next door to us was one of the best things about living where we did. Nana liked spending time with the boys and managed to keep them busy. Nana and Pop Pop bought the house next to the one Dad bought for us and moved there from West Palm Beach, just one week after we moved in. After being away for seven years, Dad moved us back to Turtle River, the town where we lived when I was born and the town where Pop Pop lived when he was a boy.

Pop Pop had always wanted to return, and it was like a zillion years since he lived in Turtle River. But now that he was there again, I think he was as disappointed as I was. He was too old, and too many things had changed. The boys were happy though, and Dad was happy teaching ceramics at the community college. But it seemed like he was never home. Even now, with Nana and Pop Pop next door, the boys depended on me, and I sometimes felt like I was caught in a web. But then, I really loved my brothers and knew I would never leave them the way Mom left all of us.

CHAPTER 3

The Trouble with Pop Pop

"I'm gonna get that guy," said Ryan.

"You're going to stay away from there, that's what you're going to do," said Nana. Nana's short, straight hair was as white as the milk she poured into the glasses set on the table at the boy's places.

"Missy, you ought to be keeping a better eye on your brothers," said Pop Pop.

I felt my stomach knot. Pop Pop had a knack for making me feel guilty.

"I think we should call the police," said Nana.

I wondered if that was such a good idea. But I saw Pop Pop, seated in his recliner by the window in the living room, already dialing. "Don't give them our names," I yelled. But filtered through the voices of my brothers and the ever going TV I heard him say his grandchildren saw it.

More than a little angry, I stared daggers at his nearly bald head with its few puffs of white hair at the very back. I remembered Pop Pop's first impression of Doyle was of a "nice-looking young fella, with a decent haircut." Of course he had changed his opinion since then.

The aroma of pizza filled the room. I helped Nana put the open boxes on the table, and I remembered I was hungry. I sat down, grabbed a cheese oozing slice and pushed my dread and anger aside.

"Come on Pop Pop," yelled Richie.

Pop Pop sat at his place, where Nana set a hamburger on a plate. He couldn't eat pizza—his digestive system— and he never ate very much of anything, which I guessed was why he stayed so skinny. But then most of us Vicellies were skinny. Nana was short and round—but she was born a Robbins.

"Tomorrow we'll have a picnic at the park by the beach," Nana announced, as she pulled up her chair. Nana, ten years younger than Pop Pop, was full of energy and always ready for a trip to the beach.

"Do you think Dave could come with us for a change?" asked Pop Pop. "Maybe that spring chicken he was out with last week will come along." He snorted and shook his head. "If she wore her dresses any shorter we'd—"

"Stop that Fritz," interrupted Nana. "If he wants to bring her, that's just fine."

"She's a bimbo," I said.

Nana gave me a sharp look. "Your Dad has to have some kind of a social life away from us."

I looked at Pop Pop and suddenly become aware of what he was eating. "That's not a hamburger, that's one of my veggie burgers," I said. But Pop Pop wasn't listening; his attention was on the evening news.

"Since when has he started eating veggie burgers?" I asked Nana.

She giggled and put some salad on Ryan's plate. "Since he's discovered he likes the flavor," she said.

Suddenly I couldn't help myself and started to laugh. He always made remarks about my "special food" because I was a vegetarian— a matter of morals for me.

"What's so funny?" asked Pop Pop.

"Nothing," I said.

"Look at that!" he said, motioning toward the TV. "There's not a night goes by without another murder or a shooting of some sort. And nine-tenths of the time it's their kind."

"Pop Pop, you're a racist!" I said. I really hated when he talked like that.

"Now I suppose you're going to stand up for them, just like your dad," he said.

"But, Pop Pop," I said, "what about that Rebecca lady you told me about. She was black and you said you loved her almost as much as you loved your own mom."

"She was different. There aren't any like *her* around anymore. Ask your Aunt Susie. She was mugged by a couple of them last year. Landed in the hospital, lucky to be alive."

"She's okay now," said Nana. Let's talk about something else."

"I suppose you think it was one of them who murdered that cat in the woods," I said, ignoring Nana.

"Don't try to be smart," said Pop Pop, raising his voice. "I'm talking about crime on the streets."

"Stop that!" yelled Ryan.

"Listen to the child," said Nana. "Stop the arguing, and let's have pleasant conversation. Missy is going on that field trip Monday, you know?"

"What field trip?" asked Pop Pop.

"Fritz! You talk about Dave not listening."

I munched on pizza while Nana chewed out Pop Pop. He said Dad never knows what's happening in our family, which was correct. He had so many things going on in his head, it made him absent-minded. One day he even forgot to pick up Richie from soccer practice.

"Remember the canoe trip up the river Missy is going to take with her class?" said Nana.

"I remember. I just didn't know it was Monday," said Pop Pop.

Suddenly a light flashed in his eyes. He leaned back in his chair and stared into space, then clicked off the TV with the remote. "I couldn't even count the days I spent on that river and in those woods," he said.

I took a swallow of iced tea and got ready for a story. I really did love Pop Pop, and missed him in the years we lived in Pennsylvania. Even though we seemed to clash about things now, I knew he had a lot of stories to tell about his childhood, and I was always ready to hear them. He lived in a house that still sat right on the widest part of the Turtle River, and he loved to drive us by to see it. He said none of us could afford that house today. The river now had become a place for the rich.

"That river used to be full of turtles," Pop Pop said. "That's where it got its name. And back then the snook— that fish we love to eat— were stacked up like cordwood under the old railroad bridge, and the mullet were so thick you could almost walk on 'em."

"I want to see something on this trip," I said. "I wish I could see something big, like a panther."

"Used to be panther in those woods," said Pop Pop. "Not anymore." He shook his head. "I'll go to my grave regretting the years I spent in real estate. I did my part to sell off our state."

"Don't be so hard on yourself. You had to make a living," said Nana.

"I'll tell you," Pop Pop said, ignoring Nana. "I'll tell you about one trip up the river I'll never forget. Didn't see any panther that time, but I saw an old Seminole hermit who lived in a chickee right next to a pair of great horned owls and one little owlet.

"What's a chickee?" asked Ryan.

"We learned about that in school," said Richie. "It's a Seminole house. "It's like a platform with four posts and a roof made of palm fronds.

"Very good, Richie," said Nana.

"The Seminole don't usually take to owls," said Pop Pop, as if he'd never been interrupted. "But this old guy, he talked to them. And legend was they talked to him." Pop Pop looked at each of us.

"Cool," said Ryan through a mouthful of pizza.

I felt a tingling run down my spine. This was weird. Pop Pop telling this story after that odd feeling I had when I looked at Caleb's drawing today. Coincidence or something else?

CHAPTER 4

Pop Pop's Story

"I reckon I was just about Missy's age," said Pop Pop "Four of us took Ernie's motor boat up river, intending to find a place to camp and fish. We stumbled into that old Seminole's place by accident, and he was right hospitable to us. He let us camp just around the bend from his chickee, where he said was the best fishing place. We caught a bunch of them too. We made ourselves a lean-to from palm fronds, built a fire and cooked the fish."

"What's a lean-to?" asked Ryan.

"Stop interruptin'," said Richie.

Pop Pop smiled. "It's a shelter. We strung a line between two trees and leaned branches and palm fronds against it."

"Skeeters were real bad and we smothered ourselves with citronella, but a whole lot of scratching was going on in the lean-to that night."

"Next morning I woke and discovered one of us—James LaRue—was missing. He was older than the rest of us, and as big a jerk and bully as ever was. I never did trust that guy, so I got myself up and went to look for him. That's when I discovered what I did."

Pop Pop just stared into space, like he was looking at something only he could see. "LaRue was headed down the path toward Brother Owl's. I followed him into the old Seminole's yard, and I saw him crawl under the tree branches to where the owls' nest was. Before I could do a thing, I heard a shot, and next thing I knew he was out of there with the owlet in a bag."

"What a rotscum!" Richie said.

"He was scum all right." Pop Pop folded his arms and shook his head. "Just as the sun was reddening the morning sky, he was ready to take off with the owlet in Ernie's motor boat and leave the rest of us behind. I got to the dock just in time and jumped into the boat to try and stop him. He got up and pushed me, I grabbed him, and we both fell into the water. He got the best of me. Held my head under till I swallowed so much water, I thought I was going to drown right then. But, all of a sudden, LaRue let go. I came to the surface, spitting water and gasping for air. Heard screaming. Opened my eyes and saw LaRue attacked by the biggest doggone owl I'd ever seen!"

"Then what?" asked Ryan, his eyes wide and looking very owl-like himself.

Pop Pop looked at Ryan and took a swallow of ice tea.

"LaRue and I made it to the beach. That owl flew over to the old Seminole, who was standing there. It sat right on his shoulder. At that point, LaRue pulled out a gun and aimed it toward the Seminole and the owl. That's when I dove into him. Head butted him and knocked his gun from his hand."

"Go, Pop Pop," said Richie, raising his fist in the air.

I saw Nana smile with a closed mouth, chewing on a piece of pizza.

"That LaRue was down, but not just because I pushed him," said Pop Pop. "No, that owl came after him a second time, and LaRue was done for after that."

"Did it kill him?" asked Ryan.

"Nah. But he was pretty bloody and cut up and durned near scared to death. That was one big owl. It took away his desire to go back into those woods," Pop Pop said, shaking his head.

"Awesome!" said Richie.

"I'm glad that creep got what he deserved," I said.

"And Pop Pop saved the owlet," said Ryan.

"I gave the owlet back to the old Seminole, and the big owl flew back to his shoulder. And then we left," said Pop Pop. "The next day Ernie and his daddy went up the river to see him, but he was gone. And so were the owls. Not a sign of 'em."

Pop Pop picked up his veggie burger, then stopped. He shook his head. "Mysterious things happened on that river back then. Been thinking a lot about those days— think those owls appreciated what I did for them. There came a couple of times after that, when an owl would appear to me— usually just when a change was about to occur in my life."

"What do you mean,' I asked.

But Pop Pop just stared down at his burger and slowly lifted it to his mouth. Richie took another piece of pizza, and Ryan pushed his chair back.

"Eat your salad and you can have dessert," I heard Nana say.

I thought I'd like to tell Pop Pop about Caleb and his drawings, but I thought better of it. Pop Pop being the racist he was the less he knew about Caleb the better.

CHAPTER 5

Partners on the River

It was early morning. I could see Mr. Rosenberg (or Mr. R., as everyone called him) from my bus window as he waited for the last of the students and the Asher Park biologist, Sandra Black, to arrive. Mr. R. reminded me a lot of Dad. He was tall and giraffe-like, in khaki shorts and a blue t-shirt, and he had grey-brown hair that started way back on his head.

Sandra Black was in charge of the students on the second bus. Canoes were stacked on the trailer attached to the back of our bus and ready to take us to River's End Park, where we would launch them and canoe to a place called Rendezvous. Those on the other bus were going to Asher Park to hike to Rendezvous. On the return trip, we'd hike and they'd canoe.

Doyle Weaver walked toward me in the aisle, and I fiddled with my backpack until he passed me. I wished that creep was with the other group.

A parent chaperone, walked by, and behind her, Beth Schier stopped and took the seat beside me.

"Hi, Missy," she said. "Are you ready for this? Have you canoed before? I haven't, and I'm a little scared."

"Sure I've canoed. Did white water in the mountains— level four."

I wasn't surprised she hadn't canoed. She was nice and all and she'd been friendly to me, but she was way too wimpy for me to want her as a close friend.

From the window I saw Caleb and Joshua arrive.

"Hey, Joneses! Last, as usual!" Mr. R. smiled as they come toward him. He waved goodbye to Sandra Black.

"Meet you at Rendezvous!" She called before she got into her bus.

Mr. R. followed the guys into our bus. Caleb smiled at me when he passed, which made my heart accelerate. I had some kind of feeling I couldn't quite explain about him.

"Maybe we'll be partners," said Beth as the bus pulled away. "You're the experienced one and I'm the novice. Mr. R said he's going to pair us together that way."

God, I hope she's not my partner. The way she yammers on in that baby voice. It drives me crazy. But then, what if Mr. R. makes Doyle my partner? He wouldn't. No, Doyle's had experience. He won't be with me.

"I was at River's End with my family for a picnic one Sunday," Beth said. "It was so crowded we almost didn't find a table. And the number of people canoeing was unbelievable! It really is a good thing Mr. R. planned this for a weekday when there aren't so many people around."

"Umm." I felt an uneasiness grow inside me. *Why didn't Mr. R. let us know our partners ahead of time?*

When we reached River's End, Mr. R., the chaperone, Caleb and another guy took the canoes down. When they finished, Mr. R. took his roll sheet from a pocket and begins to call out our names. I felt my palms grow clammy.

He read off the names of the kids who would be partnering and when he came to Beth he said she was with him, and then there were only a few of us left— I held my breath. "Missy is with Caleb. *" I can't believe it! Caleb's my partner!* My heart leapt and I silently cheered.

We all picked canoes and dragged them down a slope to the dark tannin-colored water, one canoe at a time. The sun was bright and it was hot. I had on my sunglasses, I slathered myself with coconut scented sun screen, then put on my baseball cap. My skin was so sensitive to the sun I needed every bit of protection I could get. Once when I was really young, Mom left me out on the beach too long, and I got so burned they had to take me to the hospital. Maybe that's why I didn't care to just sit on the beach. Even so, I was happiest when I was outside, surrounded by nature.

Mr. R. reminded us again to go quietly and we might see something. But soon the chaos of this many people on the river at one time made me doubtful we'd see anything but each other.

Somehow Caleb and I were the last to push away from shore. He was in the front and I was in the back, which meant I would do the steering. I learned from the start he had no experience with a canoe. None at all! I had to teach him how to paddle and get coordinated with me, and that made me feel good, to be better at something than Caleb was.

The narrow, twisting river was different from what I was used to in Pennsylvania. Caleb and I laughed when we bumped into logs and scraped against hanging branches, and we could see the others through the trees ahead of us doing the same thing. Someone splashed into the water and Joshua's voice echoed through the corridor.

Eventually the river widened some, Caleb began paddling almost like a pro, and we developed a slow rhythm. Only a little light came through the awesome canopy made by a jungle of tall trees. Many, I knew, were the giant cypress trees. It was a hot day but under the shade of the trees it felt cooler. Translucent-winged dragonflies dove through the air, and one landed on me and tickled my skin, bidding me welcome to its green cathedral. There was a shriek of a bird and the dim echoes of the other canoeists as their paddles banged against their boats. The fragrant smell of sweet flowers was in the air.

Caleb pointed at a painted turtle sitting on a log that splashed into the water on our approach. Further along, he pointed at a small gator near the bank, barely visible, but for his eyes. Not like the one I saw the other time— before Richie and Ryan were born.

On that trip I sat in the middle of the canoe between Mom and Dad. I was watching for critters to appear between the trees, expecting to see one of the panthers or bobcats Pop Pop talked about. Then, we rounded a bend and a gator as long as our canoe splashed into the water in front of us. Mom screamed, and I sat petrified, sure it would overturn our canoe and eat us. But that gator sank deep into the water, and we didn't see it again. It was a long time ago that we shared that experience.

There came a PING, PING. A hard rain was bouncing off the water and in a moment it was running off our hats. We steered under a canopy of thick vines and listened to the rain's beat. But as soon as it began, it was over, and now the sun created glowing, lacy patterns on the river. A faint putrid smell of muck passed through the air.

Caleb shook the rain from his hat and we paddled again. I looked into the trees and felt the power of the awesome place. I thought of Caleb's drawings. "Have you ever been here before?" I asked him.

"Not on the water like this."

"Well, all those crawling vines and branches make me think of your drawings."

Caleb didn't say anything, but I started to talk. I told him about the other time I was on the river, and then I told him about how my Pop Pop used to roam the woods. I couldn't believe I was talking that much, but I didn't stop. I told him Pop Pop's story about the owl family and the Seminole. All the while I was talking and paddling, when suddenly Caleb stopped and turned around to face me. His hat shadowed his eyes, and I couldn't imagine what he was thinking.

"A man who talks to owls." I laughed, "and they talk back."

A hawk called nearby. I felt stupid.

"Well it's only a story my Pop Pop told," I said, and wished I had never brought it up. I began paddling again and so did Caleb.

"Owls talked to me too," he said suddenly.

CHAPTER 6

Secrets

I felt my heart jump. "What did you say?"

"Owls talked to me."

"Get outta here. You're kidding. I told you it was just a crazy story of my Pop Pop's."

"No," said Caleb. "That story gives me goose bumps. It first happened to me when I was five years old. I was at Asher Park with my family for a reunion. I went wandering into the woods alone and I got lost."

"Well, that must have been scary."

Caleb stopped paddling again, put the paddle over his legs and glanced back at me. I stopped paddling too, and he turned in his seat so I could see his profile.

"I kept walking and walking," he said. "But I was off the path and going the wrong way. When my family realized I was gone, it was getting to be dark. They didn't find me till next morning, far away from where we picnicked."

"Sheez, you must have been really scared."

"Yeah. . . especially when it got dark . . . until *they* came."

"Who?"

"Four little owls. I remember counting them," said Caleb. "They sat in the trees around me and told me not to be afraid."

"Now *I* have goose bumps. This is crazy!"

"It wasn't exactly a voice. It was a voice inside me, but I knew it was coming from the owls. It said not to be afraid, and somehow I knew everything would be okay. And there was a kind of glow around them—like a lamp light. They stayed 'till just before I was found."

"Get out. That's too much."

"It's true," he said.

"So, presuming this is true, I suppose that's why you draw owls?" He nodded.

"How many other people know about this?"

"I haven't done any talking about it since right after it first happened."

We were drifting up against the shore. I pushed us away, started to paddle again, and Caleb followed. "Does Joshua know?" I asked.

"No. The only person who knows is my daddy."

"And now me," I added. "What does your daddy say about it?" I asked.

"My daddy's a preacher," said Caleb. "He knows about spiritual things, but he never wanted me to talk about what I saw. I'm not sure he even believed me."

"YO MISSY! YO CALEB!"

"OVER HERE!" yelled Caleb.

I had almost forgotten all about the others. "Guess we're getting behind," I said. We concentrated on our paddling and soon the river widened and we could see the others far ahead of us. There was a breeze at our back that allowed us to pick up our pace and keep a steady rhythm. We followed the others into a narrow branch of the river, and then lost sight of them. We knew we were near Rendezvous when we heard voices again, and we heard the canoes banging against the docking ramps.

When we got to the dock Caleb tied our canoe to a post, and we climbed a path leading to the top of an embankment. "Why ya'll so slow?" asked Joshua from the top. He wolfed down half a sandwich.

Mr. R. was sitting at a table, along with a park ranger, the parent chaperone and three kids— among them, Beth. "I was afraid you two were going to get lost back there," said Mr. R. "The hikers aren't here yet, and the others are out doing some exploring." He opened a cooler and motioned for us to help ourselves to drinks. "Eat your lunches, and look around."

"Come on, this place is hot," said Joshua. Caleb took a diet coke and held the cooler open for me. I grabbed a ginger ale and followed him and Joshua along a sandy trail that led away from the river and into a stand of pine trees.

"Hey! Look at that gopher!" Joshua howled and pointed to a gopher tortoise hurrying along the path ahead of us.

I came close and saw a piece of grass hanging from its mouth, and I laughed. "We must have interrupted its dinner," It stopped and pulled its head into its shell.

"Our daddy used to eat those when he was a boy," said Joshua. I remembered Pop Pop talking about eating gopher turtles, too. *Thank Heaven they're protected by laws now.*

"Come on," called Caleb. "Leave it alone."

We walked on until we spotted a fallen tree, where we sat. I took out my trail mix, Caleb pulled his sandwich from his backpack, and Joshua walked around poking into bushes and guzzling his soda.

We heard someone coming from around a bend in the trail. Doyle Weaver looked at us and curled his lips into a smirk when he passed. We heard others approach from where Doyle had come. A girl screamed, another one laughed and Joshua headed toward them.

"We're not going to see much on this trip, except for them," said Caleb, pointing to a couple of squirrels watching us from a tree.

Soon a group of kids came our way, with Joshua among them. "Hey Caleb," said one of the girls as they passed by. Then all was quiet.

Caleb threw the last bite of his sandwich to the squirrels and took his sketch book from his backpack. I watched him sketch what he saw, amazed at how easy it was for him.

"Let me draw you," he said, suddenly, turning my way. "I need a woodland elf in the picture."

"What?" I felt my face get hot. "Real funny. "You're making fun of my ears," I said and turned away from him.

"Wooh. Come on. I meant it in a nice way. The way your eyebrows rise at an angle. And the way your nose turns up. . . it's elf-like." He laughed. "And I guess your ears too, a little bit." .

I looked at him and he covered his mouth with his hand and laughed some more. I knew he really did mean what he said in a nice way. *Maybe it's not so bad to have ears that stick out a little*, I thought.

"Just look over at those squirrels," he said, pointing to my left. "I'll catch your profile."

"Okay. But you better make me look good."

"Don't worry."

After a couple of minutes of sketching the hikers appeared on the trail with Sandra Black, and Caleb closed his book and put his pencils away while we waited for them to pass.

"Let me see what you did to me," I said. He showed me. It was just my head and shoulders, but it really did look like me, and I didn't look bad.

"Elfin," he said, and laughed.

"Ha, ha," I said. We both got up and followed the others back to the river.

I walked behind Caleb and I remembered the gopher tortoise and stopped to look around for it. I almost missed it, then I spotted it about eight feet off the trail, hidden among some weeds. It was on its back, struggling helplessly to turn over.

Caleb, unaware of the turtle's plight, was way ahead of me now. I trudged through the thickets over to the tortoise and turned it right side up. "You'll be okay now," I said to it and moved it a distance away, where it wouldn't be seen by anyone passing on the trail. It would have died if left on its back, and I knew it didn't get that way by itself. Someone from our class was responsible. I knew it.

What kind of person would harm a helpless animal and get some sick satisfaction out of it, I wondered. *A true scum of the earth, who would do the same to a person if he could get away with it. Someone like Doyle Weaver. Like with the bloody cat hanging from the tree.* When the police got around to looking into it, there was no evidence it had even been there. *And Doyle probably knows it was my family who made the call.*

There were people like Doyle, and then there was Caleb, who said owls came to him and comforted him when he was alone and afraid. It was really uncanny the way Caleb's story fits in with Pop Pop's. I knew Caleb didn't just make it up, and I thought it was more than a coincidence that Pop Pop had just told us that story on Friday.

CHAPTER 7

Monday Night

"MISSY, PHONE! IT'S A BOY," called Richie.

He gave off a piercing screech into the phone before I grabbed it from him and took it to my room. I closed the door and took a deep breath to try and calm my thumping heart.

"Hello?"

"Hi Missy, it's Caleb."

"Caleb. Hi. I'm sorry, I hope your ear's okay."

Caleb laughed. "What *was* that?"

"Just one of my little brothers. What a pain. And I've had to spend half my life babysitting for them."

"It's okay. I like little kids. I do things with the grade school kids from our church on some afternoons. It's when Daddy has me watching over Joshua that bugs me."

"Well, I don't blame you, he's about as old as you are."

"Yeah, just about. But Daddy wants me to keep an eye on him."

"Oh, what fun."

Caleb laughed.

"That trip down the river was pretty awesome," I said.

"Yeah, it's cool we're partners, too. I mean, what do you think about that assignment he gave us? Since you're my partner, I was calling to see how you want to do it."

He thinks it's cool we're partners. Wow! "I think—uh—I have an idea we could make a book together," I said. "I don't mind doing the research and the writing if you'll draw the pictures."

23

"Cool. I can do pictures, I'm just not much for oral reports."

"Part of it is supposed to be reflections and our own observations of the trip," I said. "I can write that out and present it, unless you want—"

"No." Caleb laughed. "You can do it."

"Well, I can do research in the school library and I can use my dad's computer and get some of the information off the Internet. We can make a book.

"Yeah. I like that. A book sounds cool. I just wish I could go to the park sometime when there isn't anyone around," said Caleb. "Maybe I could really see something to draw."

"Yeah, maybe you'd even see your owls." I said. "But then you don't need to see them. You already have a picture of them in your head."

There was a pause, then Caleb said, "Don't say anything to anybody about what I told you— about the owls— Okay?"

I thought of Ann Marie and how I might write her about Caleb. I didn't need to be angry with her anymore. I guess I was just jealous because she had moved on and I hadn't. But that was all past and now I had Caleb. No, I wouldn't tell Ann Marie about him, at least not everything. I would never betray him.

"Missy?" Caleb said.

"No," I said. "Don't worry, I won't tell anybody. And I'll write something up tonight for our report, so we can give it to Mr. R. and get our ideas in. We could even use old timers' stories, like our grandparents eating gopher meat. And listen to what my Pop Pop told me about alligators. Did you know that the female will kill and eat the male if he tries to hang around too long after they mate? Get a picture of that."

"They're cannibals!" said Caleb.

"But, she's only protecting her eggs she's about to lay." I told him. "She knows that he would eat the eggs or the baby alligators after they hatch. Female alligators are really protective mothers."

"I guess my mama would have been that protective," said Caleb. "If I had a daddy who would have eaten me."

"Not mine," I said. "She would've just gotten lost, like she did anyhow."

"It's hard not having a mom. Mine died two years ago," said Caleb.

"Missy!" Dad opened my door and stuck his head in my room. "Nana's got dinner ready."

"Oh. I'm sorry to hear about your mom. . . ah, my Dad just told me dinner is ready. I have to go."

"That's okay. I've got to fix something for us to eat. My Daddy's out visiting someone from church who's in the hospital," said Caleb.

"Well, I'll see you tomorrow," I said and hung up after he said goodbye.

He doesn't have a mom either. But to have your mom die. That must be really hard.

C H A P T E R 8

Ms. Coplan's Class

It was Monday again and critique day in Ms. Coplan's art class. Only two weeks since the field trip, but it seemed like a lifetime. Before I sat alone in the cafeteria. Now I sat with Caleb and Joshua— even though he could be a pain— and I sat with Latanya and Amber— though not so much Amber. They still reminded me of a couple of fashion dolls, but the more I got to know Latanya, the more I saw there were big differences between her and Amber— more than just black and white.

My mind wandered to thoughts of Caleb. *The project we're working on is going to be good. We only see each other at school, but we talk on the phone about the project and a lot of other things. I do most of the talking. Amazing how much I can talk when I'm around a quiet person who listens. And Caleb has a sense of humor. We both like to compare people to animals, and we get hysterical over our analogies. He still calls me an elf and I'd say he's a deer. He says he's a young buck. The thing is, Caleb's become my best friend. And I've discovered we are kindred spirits in many ways. Our birthdays are one day apart in August— only I just turned 13, he turned 14. We both don't have mothers and—*

"Missy. Missy. Helllooooo."

"Yes!" I snapped to attention when I realized Ms. Coplan was talking to me.

She looked at me with smiling blue eyes.

"Where were you? Not here."

Caleb, sitting next to me, snickered. But I didn't mind.

"We're ready to critique your painting," said Ms. Coplan. "I like what you've started. You've loosened up in the past couple of weeks. Your drawing was so tight, maybe working with paint has brought you out. Whatever it is, keep it up."

Ms. Coplan pushed strands of long black hair away from her face and pointed to my painting. "Someone tell me what feeling you get when you look at this painting?"

"Motion," said Latanya. "Kind of quivering, like."

"Exactly," said Ms. Coplan. "The horse and rider give us a feeling of movement in an organic sense. A sense of being alive. I like that."

It was funny, but alive was exactly how I'd been feeling— more alive than I'd felt in a long time. So alive, it was scary. Like I wasn't allowed to feel that good and something was bound to come along and ruin it.

Ms. Coplan was already moving on to Caleb's work. "Caleb," she said. I like the simplicity you have here, and besides being able to draw magnificently, you show a great sense of color."

"Aw, come on," moaned Joshua. "You're gonna give him a big head."

Ms. Coplan ignored Joshua and continued to critique Caleb's work. "You stick with this. Anyone have anything to say about this painting?"

"It's awesome," said a nose-ringed boy with long dyed-black hair.

"It is getting there," said Ms. Coplan, looking at Caleb.

The critique was finished and everyone returned to his or her seat. Ms. Coplan was standing over Caleb, thumbing through his sketchbook. "Caleb!" she said. "When did you do these drawings?"

"Those are for my project in Mr. R's class," he answered.

Ms. Coplan looked at his drawings of a squirrel— the ones he started when we were in the park. She smiled. "Mr. R. has gotten you moving into new directions," she said and she turned the pages and studied the drawings of otters and alligators. "And here's Missy. She looks like an elf." Caleb gave me a fleeting look, then looked down and laughed.

"You know Caleb," said Ms. Coplan, "I'm counting on you to be one of my top art students. I like the new work in your portfolio. Your owls are wonderful, and so is that painting you've started, but I like seeing you try new subject matter."

Caleb smiled, and looked embarrassed, avoiding Ms. Coplan's eyes. At the next table over, Doyle Weaver, who was sitting between Joshua and Amber, smirked and whispered something in Amber's ear. He was supposed to be at lunch, but for some reason Ms. Coplan had been allowing him in the art room lately.

Suddenly he laughed out loud, and at the same moment Joshua sailed a book across the room. Ms. Coplan looked up in time to see the book hit the cabinet with a thud.

"Doyle, I told you that you can stay in here as long as there are no problems."

"Hey! I didn't throw that," he said, and added a few curse words that make Ms. Coplan raise her eyebrows.

"I think it's time for you to leave." she said.

"I didn't do anything!" he shouted. "He did it." He pointed to Joshua.

"Leave now!" Ms. Coplan pointed to the door.

Doyle got up and I heard him say, "Bitch," under his breath when he passed by me.

CHAPTER 9

Friends and Enemies

I saw Beth come into the cafeteria. I'd been feeling guilty about the way I blew her off when she wanted to be my friend, and the day before I'd asked her if she'd like to sit with us. But she turned me down— said she has her own friends to sit with. Maybe she didn't like being around blacks, or maybe she didn't like me anymore. I tried, I told myself. Anyhow, she reminded me of an armadillo— something about the way she walked.

Armadillo. "Hey guys, did you know armadillos are not native to south Florida?" I said to my friends at the table. "Really. They're native to South America, and they ended up here—"

"Shut-up, Missy," said Joshua, throwing a French fry at me. "I'm sick of hearing about your stupid little animals. You and Caleb. Like the stupid upside down turtle."

Latanya looked at me and rolled her eyes. "What's with you, Joshua?" she said.

"Nothing," he said. "I just got better things to talk about. Like this." He held up a flyer for everyone at the lunch table to see.

PARTY: DOYLE WEAVER'S
24 PELICAN WAY
FRIDAY NIGHT

"And I know his old man and old lady ain't gonna be there. It's gonna to be hot," Joshua said.

"I wouldn't have thought he'd invite you," said Latanya. "Not after the way you got him in trouble with Ms. Coplan yesterday."

"Got the party ticket. Amber gave it to me. All I need."

Latanya rolled her eyes again. "Oh Lord. She gave me one too."

"She's his woman," said Joshua.

"Yeah." Latanya laughed. "I don't know where her head is these days."

"Are you going to the party?" I asked Latanya.

"You crazy, girl! My mama would kill me."

"And so would our daddy," said Caleb crumpling up his sandwich paper. "A party at a rich, white boy's house is bad enough, but at Doyle's, and no chaperone…"

"I know my dad would have a real fit If I went to a party like that," I said. "But I wouldn't want to go to anything at Doyle's house, anyhow."

"Aw." Joshua shook his head in disgust.

"Come on," said Caleb. "That ain't all of it. I heard there's going to be beer there and who knows what else."

"Plus, the guy is a creep," said Latanya. "I don't know why all those white girls think he's so hot. I mean maybe he is cute, in a way, but—"

"I don't think he's hot," I interrupted. "He's reptilian." I took a sip of my milk shake and the others laughed.

"You're pretty cool, Missy," Latanya said. "You know, before I got to know you, I thought you had an *attitude.*"

"Unm., guess I did," I said and suddenly felt self-conscious, wondering if she guessed the way I thought of her and Amber.

"But you're cool now," Latanya said, bobbing her head. "Anyhow, back to Doyle. When he first moved here last year—"

"Wait a minute," I said. "He's only been here a year?"

"Who cares about any of that," yelled Joshua. "He's got a big house and a boat, and his old man and old lady won't be home. That party's gonna to be a killer."

"And we'd be looking at big time trouble if we go there," said Caleb. "I heard there's going to be older kids there from his old neighborhood."

"Doyle's the type you don't want to fool with," I said.

Joshua ignored me. "Just because you're a baby, don't mean I have to be," he said, glaring at Caleb. Then he got up and stalked away.

I watched him go, then I saw one of Latanya's friends from cheerleading wave to her.

"I got to go talk to Prissy for a minute," said Latanya. "See you guys later," she jumped up and waved us off.

"That Doyle is going to be trouble for Joshua," said Caleb.

"I agree."

Caleb stared into space for a moment. "You know what I want to do," he said, flipping his straw against his chin. "I want to go back to the park. We need more drawings for our project. I did some drawings from photographs, but I'd rather be there and get the feeling of the place."

"Well, you said that before," I said. "Why don't we do it? The county bus goes right by the park entrance. I saw it stop the day we were there. We could meet tomorrow morning at the bus stop across the street from the school."

I saw Caleb shaking his head. "Oh! Maybe you want to go alone," I said.

"No. I just don't know about skipping school," he said.

"It's the only way. Week-ends and holidays are too crowded. And there isn't enough time after school." As I spoke I realized I enjoyed the thought of doing something rebellious. "It wouldn't hurt to skip school one time," I said. "It would be our own unofficial field trip. Who knows what we might see."

The end of lunch bell rang. "I'll think about it," said Caleb, before we headed in different directions. "I'll call you tonight."

I was walking across campus—we had open campus in those days with a walkway between the two buildings. I was mentally convincing myself that my idea of skipping school was a good one, when I noticed two black girls walking toward me. One of them was enormous. Both had their eyes fixed on mine, like darts fixing on a target. I felt a sudden urge to run. *What do they want? I don't even know them.*

"Hey, Pale Face!" the big one shouted. "Stay away from Caleb." She shoved me off the walkway, hurling me onto the grass with a hard thud as I landed on my side. That hurt. I heard them both laugh as they moved on. I sat stunned for a moment, then started to pull myself together. Other students passed by, but no one said anything or moved to help me.

And I avoided looking at anyone, until I heard a friendly voice. "Missy!" Latanya was at my side. "You okay, girlfriend? What happened?"

I got up and she helped me with my backpack. She had called me girlfriend, and that felt good.

"I'm okay," I said. "Just embarrassed."

"So what happened?"

"See those two girls standing next to that Travis kid?" I pointed down the walkway toward the patio. "The big one told me to stay away from Caleb, and then she shoved me down."

"Ooh. Lord! Jealous sisters. Don't worry, I'll straighten them out."

"Caleb and I are only friends," I said.

"Missy, you're so funny. A lot of girls at this school think he's hot. And I think after you let me do your hair—"

"Forget it!"

She raised her hands in the air, jingling her gold bracelets and I gave her a sharp look. "Okay, I'm cool." she laughed. "Anyhow, I've known Caleb since we were little kids, and he's different from most anyone else. It's like he's from another planet sometimes. Maybe it's because his daddy's a preacher. Know what I mean?"

"I guess so. But that seems to have a different kind of effect on Joshua."

"There you go." Latanya laughed again. But her mood changed as she gazed across the lawn.

I followed her gaze and saw Amber and Doyle walking together. He had his arm locked around her.

"Man," said Latanya. "What does she see in him? I think he's messing with her head. She missed cheering practice twice last week because of him. And where was she at lunch?" Latanya curled her lips down, then she gave me a high five. "I gotta go, girlfriend, or I'll be late for Spanish class, and that nada be good. Oh, and wish me luck, I'm trying out for a play in the drama room this afternoon."

"Yeah, good luck," I said, and headed in the opposite direction, to English class. I still felt shaken by my fall and the hateful looks in those girls' eyes. Latanya didn't seem to be worried, but she wasn't the one they were after. I didn't know why they felt threatened by me, anyhow. Like Amber once said, people thought I looked like a boy. And I really didn't want a boyfriend. I didn't want to end up being like Mom. Caleb was my friend— a good friend. But, I supposed it was my luck, just when I had friends like him and Latanya, I'd start collecting enemies too.

Skipping School for Asher Park

"That was easy," I said to Caleb, when we got off the bus in front of the park. The hardest part was convincing Caleb it would be okay to do this. I mean everyone has to skip a day of school once in a while. No big deal.

Dad had dropped me off at the school on his way to work. I lived too close to the school to be a bus rider, but too far to walk—at least the way Dad saw it. On this morning I waited just inside the school's entrance until Dad's car was out of sight. With all the students arriving and milling around, no one noticed me walking away. I was relieved to find Caleb at the bus stop. When we got on the bus the bus driver acted kind of weird— kept staring at us.

At the gate house just inside the park entrance, the park ranger said "Good morning. Going to do some drawing?"

We kept our sketch books out of our backpacks just so it would be clear why we were going to the park.

"We're working on a school project and hoping to find some good subjects to draw," I said.

Caleb flipped his sketchbook open and showed the ranger some of his work.

"Very impressive," the ranger said. "Good day to be outside, too." If he had any suspicions, it didn't show.

Except for one lone man fishing on the river dock, the picnic area, with its pavilion, tables and soda machine, was empty of people. We decided to take the trail that started just to the left of the parking lot that led to a lake.

We stuffed our sketch books into our backpacks. A slight breeze cooled us while we walked the trail which cut through thick sable palms that reached just inches over our heads. Soon I saw a doe ambling along just ahead of us. Caleb and I glanced at each other and picked up our pace to stay with her. She stopped, quivered her ears, and like a graceful ballerina, leapt into the palms and out of sight. Caleb leapt, too, and pretended he was going to leap right on after her.

"Now that's cool," said Caleb.

"There were plenty of deer around our house in Pennsylvania," I said. "They're beautiful and much bigger than these deer. I don't see how anyone can kill them."

"Me either," Caleb added.

We got quiet and I listened to the sounds of locusts and nearby birds. Caleb whistled to imitate a mocking bird, and it whistled back. I wished I could whistle, but I never could. I watched a butterfly flutter in front of us. It lifted up to meet with a mate, and flew into the cerulean blue. "The park ranger was right, it is a good day to be outside," I said.

After passing into a stand of pines, the path led us through swamp maples to a shallow creek. "Look at the brown color of this water," I said. "Remember what Mr. R. said. The brown is from the tannin that comes from the *profuse* vegetation dropping into the water."

"You're going to ace this course," said Caleb, laughing.

More swamp maples until we finally made it to the lake, and there were groups of cypress trees. We got our drawing materials ready, kicked off our shoes, sat on a thick clump of raised roots dangling our feet in the water. White ibises were in the trees and a heron waded in shallow spot out in the lake. Caleb hurried to sketch another heron that walked along the shore pecking in the sand. Not long after that a doe came to the lake and stopped about twelve feet away from us.

Is she the same one we saw before? I wondered, as I watched her take a long drink, then pause, lift her head, and in one timeless moment look at us before she bounded away. Caleb was rapidly sketching to capture it all. I felt a twinge of envy.

"You can draw whatever you want and it's good," I said. "It doesn't have to be owls."

Caleb smiled.

"So. . . where do you think you were when you saw the owls you told me about?" I asked.

He took out his watercolor tin, dipped his brush into the lake water, then into the blue paint which he moved across the paper. "I saw the owls two times," he said.

"You saw them again?"

"Yup. I saw them two years ago— after our house burned down," Caleb stopped painting and stared at the paper. "And after Mama died."

"That must have been a horrible time," I said, and I felt weird.

He leaned over and washed his brush in the lake again. "Yup."

I waited for what seemed a long while. He glided more blue paint across his paper.

"After the fire, our church family got us a trailer," he went on. "Supposed to be for just awhile, 'till the new house was built, but then the accident happened." He spoke softly, I leaned forward and strained to hear him.

"Mama went to the store one night. . ." He smashed his paint brush onto his paper. Hit by a drunk. I'll never forget that night. The knock on the door. It was like everything stopped. Nothing's been the same since that night." He bit down on his lower lip and stared out at the water.

"I'm sorry," I said and blinked away a tear. I wanted to go over and hug him, but I was too shy.

"Daddy didn't care about the house after that. All of us miss Mama."

"It's a terrible thing," I muttered. I'd been so busy feeling sorry for myself, telling him all about my problems, not realizing how hard his life had been. He couldn't ever see his mom again. Not ever.

Caleb leaned back against a tree and lowered his eyes. "One day my sister and her husband were visiting, and we came to this park for a picnic. It was sunny, like today, but I was feeling really depressed, like I just wanted to be alone away from everyone. I took a walk alone in the woods behind the picnic tables. Just after I'd gone a little ways in, I heard music."

"Music?"

"Yeah. It was like flutes, to the tune of *Amazing Grace* — Mama's favorite song. It was coming from someplace above me. I looked up into the trees, and had to squint my eyes because the sun was coming through the leaves. But still I could see them in the branches. Four little owls."

"You're saying owls were making music?"

"I don't know. Just…I heard the song coming from above. I could make out the whole first verse, then it started fading away."

"So, what about the owls? What happened to them?"

"They seemed to melt into the sunlight, and my sadness went with them. I remembered Mama telling me— after the first time I saw the owls— that they were really angels I saw."

"Maybe they *were* really angels," I said, hugging my knees, feeling prickly and strangely lifted. "Your guardian angel owls."

"Ever since I was little Mama loved my drawings, would make a fuss over 'em and hang 'em around the house. After I saw the owls again, that's when I started drawing nothing but owls." Caleb took out a bag of potato chips. "Let's look for a different spot," he said, offering me some potato chips.

We packed up our materials, slipped on our shoes, and started around the lake. We walked without speaking and picked our way around cypress knees that were clustered together around the water. Through the trees we saw two deer, but the cypress knees were so thick we could go no further, and we returned to the spot where we had been. While I munched on my cream cheese and olive sandwich and Caleb ate a meat loaf sandwich, I thought about everything he told me. I'd read about people having mystical experiences like that and about people who could call spirits to them. Psychics? Mystics?

"You want to see them again, don't you?" I asked.

"What?"

"The owls. Your guardian angels."

"Yeah. But I can't just make them come."

"You can," I said. "I read someplace that you can meditate on angels and spirits like that and bring them to you."

"My daddy says a person should never go looking for angels or spirits, because what he finds could likely be evil as much as good."

"What happened to you wasn't evil. Your experience was your own. But . . . this sounds weird, but I think there are strange coincidences going on. Like your owls, my Pop Pop's, and somehow I'm a part of it too. They're trying to talk to us."

"Maybe if we both tried, right here in this place," I said, "we could bring the owl spirits to us and they could talk to us— tell us things, mystical things." I stuffed my lunch wrappings in my backpack and sat cross legged on a patch of sand facing the water. I put one hand on each knee, palms up.

Caleb sat beside me on the clump of roots and bowed his head. "Ummmm. . ."

"Come on, be serious," I said.

Caleb looked at me and laughed. "Okay, Elfin, what do we do?"

"Well, let's just close our eyes and concentrate, meditate on the owls. Picture them in our minds and ask them to come."

"Okay," he said. "Let's try."

I closed my eyes and tried to picture owl spirits watching over us. I visualized owls flying and sitting in trees and asked them to appear. After what seemed a long time, nothing was happening and I started to feel silly. I pictured how we looked to someone that might come up on us, and I started to giggle. Caleb was giggling too, and then we got quiet again. After a short time an unnatural stillness seemed to surround us. Eyes closed, I silently asked the spirits to come in. I got a sudden chill when *Doyle's* face materialized before my closed eyes. I opened them and looked down into the water just in time to see a water moccasin swim by. I screamed "Snake!" and grabbed Caleb. "Let's get out of here," I said.

Caleb was already gathering his things. "Right," he said.

We followed the path back silently, glumly. *What just happened?* When I couldn't stand the silence anymore, I said "Maybe we shouldn't have done that."

CHAPTER 11

Not At This School

I awoke suddenly from a dream I couldn't remember to darkness and a ringing in my ears. I lay solid on my bed, one ear against my pillow, and put my hand over the other ear. The ringing stopped and I heard the usual night sounds of crickets and frogs and a distant car passing. I moved my foot and felt comfort in finding Sam at the foot of my bed. Outside my window shown a single star. I told myself it was a sign, morning would come and all would be well. I drifted back to sleep.

Something stirred in my brain and a new edginess came over me as I headed for my first class. Some kids were standing around Mr. R's door, so I figured it must still be locked. I didn't see Caleb or Joshua. *Why is everyone looking so serious, like they're all part of my mood. They're all whispering.* A girl moved away from the door and I saw it. A large, black swastika spray painted right in the middle of the door.

"It's awful," said Beth. "Why would anybody do that?"

The others stood around and commented and my mind swirled. I felt anger, but also had the disturbing thought that I knew something bad was going to happen today.

"Mr. R.'s Jewish," someone said.

"Wooh! Like we don't know that."

"Yeah, and I'll hate to be here when he sees this!"

"Stop that," yelled Beth. The others looked at her like she was weird. "Mr. R. is one of the nicest teachers we have," she said.

I could see that behind her thick glasses tears were forming in her eyes.

"What's your problem?" a girl standing next to Beth asked. "We all like Mr. R."

But we all knew there was someone who didn't. Someone who would do something mean like this. More students came to the door and the outrage grew louder. "Who would do that?"

Mr. R. finally arrived, and I saw the back of his neck turn crimson as he paused in front of the door. He unlocked it, opened it, and told us to be seated and he'd be right back. Then he disappeared into the hallway.

The room was buzzing.

"We don't have any skinheads at this school."

"Who says it has to be skinheads?"

Everyone looked confused and some were trying to pin blame on someone. Doyle, on the opposite side of the room, made a comment. I didn't hear what he said, but a couple of guys laughed, and I saw other kids look at him in disgust.

Neither Joshua nor Caleb had arrived when the last bell rang. Mr. R., after what seemed like a long time, came back into the room. He had an unreadable expression on his face, and he told us to take out our homework assignment like nothing had happened.

Suddenly the door opened and Joshua walked in. His mouth agape, he went to his seat.

Where is Caleb? I wondered.

Beth was standing. Wimpy Beth. What was she doing? She began to speak: "Mr. R., we want you to know that we feel extremely upset about wh— what was done to you. We . . . . we all appreciate you as our teacher, and if there's anything we can do. . . . to help find out who's responsible. Well, you can count on us. . . . me. . . . .to help. I just wanted you to know."

The room was silent when Beth took her seat again. Mr. R. stood motionless before us.

"Thank you, Beth," he finally said. "I don't know who is responsible for that piece of work. That kind always lurks in the dark. I didn't think it was present in this school." He stopped, closed his eyes, and rubbed his temples, then looked at the class. We'll just hope the responsible party comes up from his or her ignorance."

He picked up his notes from his desk. "Now, someone read the question and answer for number one on your homework assignment."

Mr. R. didn't say any more about the mark on the door, and the period seemed to crawl by. I was relieved when the bell finally rang. We all filed out the door, I smelled fresh paint, and along with others, took a look behind the door to see the hideous black mark was gone.

* * *

Joshua had bolted from the room so fast, I didn't get to ask him where Caleb was. Then in art class, he was gesturing wildly, telling everyone about the swastika.

Ms. Coplan's blue eyes looked fierce as she listened to Joshua.

I went up to him and asked where Caleb was.

"Sick," he said, and shrugged.

"Sick? How? I mean what's wrong with him?"

"Don't know, Missy," said Joshua. "Maybe his diabetes."

"Diabetes? Caleb?" But Joshua had nothing more to add; he was heading for the other side of the room.

I found Latanya at our table assembling her paints. "What's going on with Caleb?" I asked. "Joshua just told me he has diabetes."

"He does. He missed a whole year of school in the fourth grade. That's why he's in the same grade as Joshua."

I felt lightheaded. "Caleb doesn't look sick. And why didn't he ever tell me?"

"Chill, girl," said Latanya. "He doesn't talk about it. Lots of people don't know."

"But . . . . My God! I knew of a girl in Pennsylvania who died of. . . . they said, complications from diabetes. I didn't know her, but she was only fourteen."

"Caleb's dealing with it," said Latanya. "Just has to be careful and take his insulin. He doesn't want people to know about it. I think he's afraid of being treated different or something like that."

I didn't really hear her, I just wondered. *Why? He's so good. Why did that have to happen to him? Why didn't he tell me about it, after everything else he's told me. And what other bad thing is waiting around the corner?*

CHAPTER 12

Where Caleb Lives

By Friday we hadn't learned any more about the swastika, and Caleb was still not at school. "Do you think he's okay?" I asked La0tanya during art class. "This is the second day he's been out."

"Didn't you call him?" Latanya asked.

"Yeah, I called twice and both times I got his dad and he said Caleb was sleeping. And Joshua won't tell anything. I wish Caleb had a computer and could get on-line and we could e-mail each other."

"His dad has a computer in his office, but Caleb doesn't have his own e-mail address. I have an idea." Latanya looked at me from across the table, with a silly grin. "Why don't we go see him?"

"To his house?"

"Yeah," said Latanya. "I saw you out riding your bike on Main Street the other day, when my mom was taking me to the orthodontist. Why don't you ride over to the corner of Main and Garden after school and I'll meet you there. It's not really so far from there to his house."

"Sure," I said. "I'll do that." Latanya winked at me, and I wondered, did she know I'd been dying to see where Caleb lived.

"Four o'clock." she said.

At five minutes after four I followed Latanya down Garden Street, past a variety of houses, many small, like little cottages, some wood frame, and others of cement block. Most were surrounded by pine trees. One house had magenta-blooming bougainvillea inching all over one side, another house sat in the shade of a wide spreading oak tree with two little kids climbing in the branches.

"Hey," Latanya waved to the kids and they waved back.

We went about five blocks, then turned down an unpaved road that ended at a wall of green created by Florida holly and Australian pines growing so close together, I didn't think a breeze could slip through. At the end of the road, on the left side of the street, sat a small white stucco church with a high steeple and a cross on the top. Behind it was a large square building. On the other side of the street sat a trailer, with the burned-out foundation of a house nearby.

A ball bounced and a boy looking about ten or eleven years old shot a basket on a court next to the church. Caleb and another young boy went after the ball. Caleb captured it, shot for a basket and missed. Both younger boys hooted.

"Hey Bro!" yelled Latanya as we rode up beside the court. "What's happening?"

Caleb looked surprised. "Hey!"

"Missy and I were worried about you," said Latanya. "Joshua, the little lowlife, wouldn't tell us anything, and you were out *three* days. But then I know about the first day." Latanya gave me a knowing look.

Caleb grabbed the ball from one of the two boys and bounced it a few times before he threw it back to them. "Yesterday and this morning I didn't feel so good, but I'm better now."

Latanya laughed. "Well you better be, you're out in the sun playing B-ball." She looked at her watch. "Gotta go. Just came to show Missy where you stay. I told my mama I'd be right home."

"So this is where you live," I said, feeling a little awkward and wishing I could strangle Latanya, when I watched her ride away. She didn't tell me she was going to take off like that.

"Yup," said Caleb. "This is where I stay."

"Did you hear about what someone did to Mr. R.?" I asked.

"Yeah. Man, that's low. Whoever did that is a real dirtbag."

"I think there is one person in our class who might stoop that low. Like, does Doyle Weaver sound about right?"

Caleb sucked in his lips and nodded. "He would do that."

I heard a door close behind me and turned to see a black man with grey hair and glasses coming toward us from the back side of the church.

"Hey, Brother Jones," one of the boys from the court called.

"Good afternoon, boys," he said.

"Daddy, this is my friend Missy," said Caleb as Brother Jones approached us.

"We're doing a science project together."

"Hello, young lady," he said with a nod. He looked at me, and for a flickering moment, I felt a shade of disapproval in his eyes. Then he walked onto the court and started to talk with the boys.

"I've been doing some drawing while I've been home," Caleb said to me, seemingly unaware of any bad vibes that came from his dad. "Come over to the trailer and I'll show you."

I followed Caleb to the door of the trailer, where he turned and told me he would be right out. I found a seat on a picnic table under a tree and looked across the street to see Brother Jones looking back at me before he turned and disappeared into the church.

The trailer was good sized, but it was a faded blue and appeared old. It was not fancy, although it had a small wooden back porch with lawn chairs. Caleb came out and handed me his sketchbook. He watched me page through and stop at the sketches of the deer he started drawing in the park. I noticed details he had added since then and turned the page. "God, Caleb! This is so good."

"Don't use the Lord's name like that, Missy," Caleb said, with a dead serious look in his eyes. I felt hurt at being reprimanded by him, but I told myself it was because he was a preacher's son. I looked at the picture again.

A deer, with sad and pleading eyes, stared back at me. It stood among dark, heavy trees where shadowy figures lurked in the background. "These are really good," I repeated, "but scary."

"Turn the page," Caleb said.

I did and saw a large owl taking up about two thirds of the picture, with outstretched wings, hovering over two tiny figures— human figures—in a field below. "Are they us?" I asked and looked at Caleb who just smiled and nodded.

"These drawings are awesome," I said, and really did believe they were the best he'd done. Still, I couldn't shake an uneasy feeling that things weren't right. I wanted him to tell me about his diabetes. Why didn't he? I didn't want to ask about it, so instead I asked him about our experience in the woods.

"Caleb, you know after we tried that meditating the other day." Caleb nodded. "Well, just before we left, I had this weird feeling that something was— wasn't right. It was a spooky feeling and it gave me nightmares."

"I know. I felt it too."

So now, at least I know that much. We both felt it. But I doubt if he saw Doyle's face like I did.

CHAPTER 13

Dad & Pop Pop

I nearly tripped over Dad's suitcase when I came in the front door. The boys were in the great room down the hall where they were watching cartoons on the TV, and Dad was off to the side in the kitchen sitting at the bar talking on the phone.

"What's going on? Where you going?" I asked.

"And where have you been?" asked Dad, as he put the phone back in the cradle. "So busy you forgot I'm flying to Pennsylvania for the house closing?"

"No. I thought you weren't leaving till Sunday."

"I booked an earlier flight. I told you about it. Need to see your mother about some things too."

Just the mention of her made my stomach knot. "She still with that same guy?"

"Far as I know, they're living happily ever after." He raised his eyebrows. "Except they're both unemployed." He was being sarcastic, but still— how could he be so cool about it all?

Dad looked at me sternly and pointed to a note on the bar. "Here's a list of things to remember while I'm gone. Nana and Pop Pop will help you out."

"Okay. I know what to do. I've been in charge before." He continued to look at me, making me feel totally weird. "What? What's wrong?" I asked.

"Your English teacher called me today."

"Why?'

"She said you weren't in school Wednesday— said she saw you before school, across the street, getting on a bus with a black boy."

I felt a buzz up my spine. *Ms. Steuber is a nosy old hag.* I opened my mouth to speak, but Dad put up his hand.

"I said, 'No, you must be mistaken. My daughter wouldn't do anything like that. Not my Missy. But she proved I was the one mistaken. You *were* absent from school Wednesday." Dad's voice raised an octave. "And do I dare ask where you were going?"

"It wasn't anything wrong. We were working on a science project."

"You've always been honest with me in the past, Missy, but—"

"What are you talking about in here?" asked Richie, suddenly appearing from around the corner.

"We'll talk when I come back," Dad said, ignoring Richie and giving me another hard look before glancing at the clock on the wall. "I've got a plane to catch. Nana is taking the boys to their soccer practice, and Pop Pop is taking me to the airport. I want you to come with us, so he won't have to drive back alone."

"Okay, but you didn't tell Nana or Pop Pop about . . . . did you?"

"Tell them what?" asked Richie.

"Never mind," said Dad. To me he said, "No, and I'm counting on you not getting in trouble while I'm gone. Understood?"

"Yes."

"Now where did I put my wallet?" asked Dad as he headed down the hall.

"You're in trouble," said Richie. "What'd you do?"

I ignored him and went to my room to change my clothes.

CHAPTER 14

Time with Pop Pop

"She left you and the kids!" said Pop Pop. "That tramp shouldn't get a dime from you!"

"She's still the kids' mother," said Dad, who sat beside Pop Pop in the front seat of the car. "And she still cares about them. I ca—"

"You aren't thinking of taking her back? You're crazy if you do!"

"No, Daddy! Now watch the road, please!"

Pop Pop's driving made me nervous too. And it bothered me when he trashed Mom. I could hate her. It was my right. I didn't want her to be happy with that other guy, and I didn't want Dad to take her back, even if she wanted to come back. But even though I didn't understand Dad's attitude, I was glad he didn't trash her. I was proud he could be above that.

Pop Pop pulled the car up next to the airline terminal entrance; Dad hopped out and retrieved his bag from the trunk, while I moved from the back seat to the front beside Pop Pop. Dad leaned down to my open window. "Watch out for your brothers," he said. "I'll call you when I get there. See you Tuesday. Love you." He dashed off waving before he disappeared into the terminal.

A car honked at Pop Pop when he tried to ease into the traffic, and he grumbled about the crazy drivers.

"How's school coming, Missy?" He asked, after we got away from the airport.

"It's good."

"You must have plenty of friends here by now. I know I sure haven't seen much of you lately."

"Sorry, Pop Pop, I've been busy."

"That's all right. I'll bet, before long, you'll have a boyfriend, and you'll forget all about Pennsylvania," he said, glancing at me, making that funny face of his, where he'd raise his eyebrows, open his mouth in a half smile while he puckered his lips.

"I have some new friends," I said.

"I remembered when my family moved away from Turtle River," he went on. "I was real unhappy to be leaving my friends and leaving the river."

"I guess it was hard to leave that house you lived in."

"Dang right it was. But I soon found new friends and things to do that took up my time. I had basketball and in the spring baseball."

"Don't forget to turn up here," I said, as we approached the restaurant where he promised we'd stop on the way home.

"You like this place, huh?" said Pop Pop, putting on the turn signal.

"It was good the time Dad took us. Good vegetables." Something Pop Pop and I shared in common was a taste for well-cooked Southern vegetables. And they offered to-die-for blueberry cobbler.

I realized I was starving when we got inside and were greeted by an array of delicious smells. We sat down across from the coffee warmer. Coffee always smells so good— too bad about the taste. It was a cozy place, with a lantern on every table, a big fireplace at the end of the room, and country antiques hanging on the walls and sitting on shelves.

Our waitress was friendly and dressed in a long, ruffled, checked blue and white skirt and a white blouse. It was almost like we'd entered another time. After we ordered, Pop Pop spotted a coffee grinder on the shelf above us, which he said was just like the grinder his mama had.

Being here with him— just the two of us— reminded me of when I was little, before the boys were born, when I used to visit him and Nana, and I would sit by him and listen to his stories while Nana was busy with other things. Grumpy as Pop Pop could be, he came to life in a cheerful way when he told his stories.

"Thank yuh," said Pop Pop, to our waitress when she set our iced tea on the table.

"I've been thinking," I said and stirred sugar into my tea. "About those owls you saw. Did you ever see them again? The ones that talked to the Seminole."

"No. I told you Ernie Hale's Pop went up river the next day and didn't see any sign of 'em— the Seminole or the owls."

"I know, but didn't you say you saw another owl sometime after that? Like, couldn't it have been one of the same you saw with the Seminole?"

"How would I know if I were seeing the same old owls? I know I never saw any as big as the one I saw up the river that day."

"But you said there were others."

Pop Pop took a swallow of tea. "Once there was a little screech owl I had for a pet."

"But what about the owls that came into your life when there was about to be a change? "How many times did they come? What were they like?"

"Oh for crying out loud!" Pop Pop leaned back in his chair and looked at his watch and glanced toward the kitchen. "Pretty slow back there, aren't they?" He shook his head. "I've seen a lot of owls in my lifetime," he finally said. "I do remember hearing an owl call out just after my pet rooster died. That was pretty durned eerie. And I did see one on the day we moved away from Turtle River. Early in the morning I went into our yard alone and walked down by the river. I guess I was saying good-bye to the place. While I stood there I felt I was being watched."

"I know that feeling," I said.

"I turned my head," Pop Pop went on, "and there it was, sitting on a tree branch, eye-balling me. It looked at me for a long moment, then flew up, circled the house and landed on the roof. It stayed there until Mama came out the back door a little while later."

"Maybe owls are your spirit protectors."

"If they were protectors, they sure weren't there at Normandy."

I knew Normandy was where the American soldiers landed on the shores of France during World War II. It was where a lot of American guys died, and where Pop Pop lost his eye and nearly lost his leg. "Things could have been worse," I said. "If you had died, Dad, me, Richie and Ryan wouldn't be here."

"That's an awful thought, isn't it?" he said.

We sat without saying anything for awhile. Pop Pop hadn't had an easy life. He was all set for a career in baseball until *The War* messed up his chances, and now that old leg injury was giving him a lot of pain.

"Pop Pop," I said, "there's a boy at school who's always drawing owls, and he's really good at it. Anyhow, he told me about four owls that came to him in the woods, twice. They're really spirits of owls, he believes. He made me promise not to talk about it to anybody, but I just want to know what you think."

Pop Pop looked at his watch. "I think if you promised him you wouldn't talk about it, then you shouldn't. I don't know about you, but I'm getting hungry. If they don't—"

Just then the waitress appeared with Pop Pop's broiled fish and collard greens, and my spinach quiche. "You must have had to go catch that fish," Pop Pop said, scowling at her. She smiled anyhow, but I felt like crawling under the table.

We both began to eat, and neither of us said any more. Sometimes he really annoyed me.

CHAPTER 15

The Party

The phone rang. It was 10:35 pm. Dad already called from Jansville, and I called Nana and Pop Pop to tell them, so I wondered *who's calling now?*

"Hello?"

"Missy, it's Caleb."

"Caleb!" *Why is he calling so late?*

"I got to go to that party at Doyle's. Joshua's there and our Grandma's in the hospital. She's real bad off. I have to find him."

"Did you try phoning Doyle's house?"

"Yeah. All I get is a busy signal. I'm gonna take my bike and go over there, but I'm not sure which house is his."

"It's the big house at the end of the street around the curve. You can't miss it. It's the only one right on the river. But why don't you stop by my house, and I'll go with you?"

"Are you sure?"

"Yeah. Two is better than one, when it comes to going there. I'm on the left side of the street, second house in. I'll be outside waiting."

"Okay. See yuh." CLICK.

I couldn't believe I had just said that. Me go to Doyle's house? Leave the boys alone? But . . . I thought it wouldn't take long. Just long enough to find Joshua and get out of there. Caleb needed me, or he wouldn't have called. The boys were asleep. They'd never know, and they'd be just fine.

I changed out of my pajamas and into my clothes then went out to the sidewalk to wait. I could hear rock music coming from the end of the street. While watching television earlier, I had heard a motorcycle roar down the street, but I didn't hear much else. Now the squeak of Caleb's bicycle came toward me, and Sam was in my window seat barking like he was a wild dog.

Nana and Pop Pop's outside light flicked on. "Quick! Over here!" I motioned Caleb toward the front door in the alcove where he couldn't be seen. "Come in a minute," I told him. "I've got to calm Sam down before we leave."

"Nuh uh! I ain't going in there!"

"Don't tell me you're afraid of a little dog! Come on!" I grabbed Caleb by the arm and pulled him into the house. As soon as he was inside, Sam stopped barking and approached him with his tail wagging and his dirty torn teddy bear in his mouth. "See, he wants to show you his bear. How can you not love a dog like that?"

RING!

I left them both at the door and went down the hall to the kitchen to answer the phone, and I knew who it was this time.

"Is everything okay? I heard Sam barking."

"Yeah, everything's fine, Pop Pop. Someone must have been walking down the street or something."

"Something's going on down around the curve. There's a lot of racket. Did you hear those foul mouthed kids walk by a little while ago?"

"No, I was in the back."

"Well, just be sure your door's locked."

"Okay. Goodnight."

"Goodnight Missy. Call if you hear anything suspicious."

I came around the corner from the kitchen and saw Ryan standing in the hallway staring at Caleb. "Who are you?" he asked.

Caleb kneeled down and smiled. "I'm Caleb."

"It's okay, Ryan," I said. "He's my friend. Now go on back to bed."

I could tell he was only half awake and probably wouldn't even remember this in the morning. "Come on," I said and walked him to his room which he shared with Richie (the soundest sleeper in the world). I kissed Ryan and tiptoed out.

"Let's wait a few minutes to be sure he's asleep," I whispered and looked to see Caleb making friends with Sam. Sam let Caleb scratch him under his chin, then decided he'd had enough and headed into my bedroom where he jumped onto my bed.

"Isn't anyone home with your brothers?" Caleb asked. "You don't have to go with me."

"But I want to," I whispered. "You shouldn't go there alone— not to that place." I didn't tell him how nervous I was beginning to feel about this. "We won't be gone long, anyhow," I said. I checked on the boys, heard their steady breathing and signaled to Caleb to head out the front door. I followed him and locked the door behind me.

The noise from the party got louder when we approached the curve in the road that led to Doyle Weaver's house. There were only five houses on the street, counting ours and Pop Pops— one across the street from Pop Pop's, and one on the other side of us. And then there was Doyle's mansion. A car nearly ran us over as it squealed its tires at the curve, and then sped past us toward Main Street. We both stared after it.

"Man, was he in a hurry," I said to Caleb.

Cars, trucks and motorcycles were parked along the road by the woods. The Weaver's house was a massive, dark grey, three story, flat-roofed fortress. With only three people living there, I didn't know why they needed so much space. We walked up the driveway, and I gazed at a round window that looked down on us like an eye set in the middle of a massive tower rising up from the center of the front of the house. On the left side of the tower were extra high, double entrance doors, and on the right side were three, double wide, garage doors. There were two dormers that jutted out at odd places from the second and third floors. To me the whole thing was hideous and even ominous looking. But I was curious about the tower.

"Man, Doyle's gotta be rich to have a house this big," said Caleb.

We walked around the vehicles parked all over the driveway and I wondered out loud, "Where did all these cars come from? How many friends does he have that drive?"

"He doesn't need friends. When there's free beer, word gets around and they come," said Caleb.

The blaring music was vibrating against the front doors. I looked at Caleb and then pressed the doorbell. Nobody answered.

"They probably can't hear it," said Caleb.

I pushed the latch. The door opened and I saw at once that the tower was an enclosed, circular staircase— stone on the inside, as well as the outside. We passed through a large foyer and found ourselves in a vast living room filled with kids I didn't know. Many were older, maybe from the high school. Some were standing; many were lying on couches or slouched over chairs. The smell of beer and smoke filled the room, and a large white rug had spilt beer all over it.

Caleb was talking, but the music spilling from the patio outside the living room was so loud, I couldn't even hear him.

I looked around the room for someone I might know, and I spotted Amber sitting alone on the floor in a dark corner. I nudged Caleb and saw him looking at her, too. We both went to her and tried to talk to her, shook her, but she just looked at us like she didn't know us. I wondered what she had in her. She was totally out of it.

We heard guys yelling above the sound of the music and turned to see one push another hard against a sliding glass door, leaving it with a large crack. Now the two guys were outside fighting on the patio, and a shouting mob crowded around them. Caleb pulled me out an adjacent door, and we dodged a can full of beer someone threw at us. I felt sick in my stomach.

"These aren't middle school kids," I said. "I don't recognize any of them, except Amber."

"Me neither. I don't know what Joshua would be doing here."

"Over there," I said. We walked to a grassy area away from the noise and commotion, where twin boys we knew from school were sprawled on the ground, smoking. They were almost as unaware of what was going on as Amber was.

"Have you seen Joshua?" Caleb asked. They just shook their heads and laughed.

"Caleb. Have you seen Doyle?" I asked.

"No"

"Isn't that strange? It's his house? Where is he?"

Caleb looked worried. "Have you seen Joshua?" He asked another guy, who I recognized from art class.

"He was here. I saw him head for the boat a while ago," said the boy, motioning toward the river.

Caleb and I walked out the long stretch of yard to the yacht docked at the Weaver's pier. It was dimly lit on the inside. It was a big boat— Dad had seen it when he was on the river with a friend, and he said it must be 40 feet long at least. Caleb and I called out for Joshua as we approached.

"Let's go see," said Caleb.

I followed him onto the boat and down into the cabin. "Oh Lord help us!" he said when he reached the bottom. I came up behind him and couldn't believe what I saw. Someone had been there, alright, and I hoped it wasn't Joshua.

The furniture was destroyed, a table was turned over with a broken leg. Chair cushions were slashed, and shattered glass from a mirror was all over the place.

"Oh, Lordy. Joshua, where are you?" cried Caleb.

I saw movement at the window above us and grabbed Caleb's arm. An enormous owl was peering in at us, but in a flash it was gone. After that I realized everything was quiet— no music, no voices. Then there came the sound of running feet.

"Let's get out of here!" I said.

We emerged from the yacht and walked straight into a policeman with Doyle standing at his side.

CHAPTER 16

Unforgiven

"I can't go to the police station!" I heard myself wail. "My little brothers are home alone!" The police officer hand cuffed Caleb, opened the car door and pushed him in. He directed me to the other side. I started to cry. "Calm down, girl. Calm down. You say you live at the end of this street. Get in and I'll take you there." He didn't cuff me.

The back seat was separated from the front by a wire screen, and the car smelled of cigarette smoke. "We didn't do anything," I said, as he closed the door. Caleb sat mute, staring straight ahead.

The porch light was on when the police car's lights shone into our driveway, and the front door opened. "Who's that?" the officer asked.

"My Pop Pop."

The officer got out of the car, opened the door for me to get out, then closed it again.

I walked around to the other side on legs of rubber and faced Pop Pop.

"Missy! What's going on here?"

"She was found at the party down the street," the officer answered for me and took out his pad. "She and the boy in the car were found together on the Weaver family's yacht—"

"You mean she was with that coon?" Pop Pops face contorted into a hateful expression.

I felt horror, and I looked at Caleb behind the closed window. He didn't turn his head toward us. Did he hear?

"I'll release her into your custody," the officer said and I rushed past Pop Pop for the house.

"We didn't do anything wrong!" I turned and said. "And I'll never forgive you, Pop Pop!"

Sam danced around me when I came in the door. I pushed him away. Nana appeared at the end of the hallway and the boys came up beside her. The light from the great room shone behind the three of them, so I couldn't see their faces.

"I can explain," I said.

"The boys were scared to death when they woke and found you gone," Nana said. "Ryan went upstairs looking for you, and now he has a big knot on his head from a fall. I never thought you'd do a thing like that. Sneaking out of the house . . ."

"I can—" My voice cracked and a sob escaped. I ran into my bedroom and closed the door behind me. Outside my window I could see the blue lights from the police car and Pop Pop talking to the officer. He signed a paper then came into the house.

"What in the hell got into her?" I heard him yell. "She's going to end up a tramp like her mother!"

I rushed to my bedroom door and locked it. Locking Pop Pop out of my room and out of my life. I screamed, "I hate you! I wish you were dead!"

CHAPTER 17

Misery

It was eleven o'clock by the time I got out of bed the next morning. I felt sick in my stomach as I remembered the night before. The house was quiet now, and I guessed the boys must still be at their soccer games with Nana and Pop Pop. Earlier I heard Nana knock on my bedroom door and call to me once, but I told her to go away. She said for me to stay home and she'd talk to me later. Of course she had called Dad, and then he called me. I was grounded for the week-end, something which had never happened to me before. But then, where was I going to go anyhow?

I sat at Dad's computer and stared at the screen and at the information I found on the Internet. I wanted to know about the owls. Why did I see that owl in the boat's window? The Internet site said *"Owls have been a symbol of death in many cultures around the world throughout history."* Caleb's owls were good and comforting. Could owls be comforters sometimes and at other times portend death? Latanya had called me and said Caleb's grandma died during the night. Was that owl portending her death? Caleb saw it too, I think. Before Latanya called, I tried and tried to get Caleb on the phone, but it was either busy, or it kept ringing and no one answered. I really needed to talk to him, but now I knew why I couldn't get him.

I could hardly get to sleep that night. I kept seeing Caleb in that police car, with Pop Pop shouting his ugly words from outside. I had to know if Caleb heard what Pop Pop said. But how could he not have heard? What was he thinking about me? I wished I could talk to him and at least apologize. Someone came by in the morning and took his bike from the front of our house.

"*The Mayan God of Evil was the great horned owl. He was thrown down from heaven and took revenge by harming mankind,*" it said on the Internet. Maybe it depended on the kind of owl you saw.

Was the owl I saw at the window of the yacht sending a message or was it mocking us? I didn't know.

I got off the Internet, closed down the computer, and went downstairs to see who I had just heard come in the back door. Ryan was standing by the dining room table looking at me, with a big black and blue knob on his forehead, proof of my stupid acts.

"Nana made lunch," he said. His eyes held mine for a few seconds, like a sad abused puppy, and then he retreated out the sliding glass door to Nana's house.

I really couldn't handle this. I watched him leave, then went to my room and flopped down on my bed and cried.

CHAPTER 18

Dad Returns

Dread was growing in me while I waited at the curb of the pickup loop. Dad hadn't said much to me on the phone, just that he'd pick me up at school on Tuesday afternoon and not to leave the house except to go to school or Nana's and Pop Pop's house.

Caleb and Joshua weren't in school Monday or Tuesday. Doyle kind of slunk around, and Amber didn't speak to me, which wasn't unusual. I noticed her hair was no longer in braids.

Rumors were flying around the school that Caleb and I were in big trouble for vandalism. For the past two days I felt like everyone was staring at me. That girl who shoved me— she passed me on the walkway and shouted "Hey, Pale Face! Heard you trashed that white boy's boat." It was like she thought I was cool now.

Mostly, I thought everyone was making fun of me. Whenever I saw a group of kids talking and laughing, I was sure they were laughing at me. It was like all the good stuff that happened to me in the past three weeks had gone into reverse.

Dad's truck pulled up to the curb, and I numbly climbed in and felt the thud of the closing car door like the blow of an ax whacking off my head. Dad gave me a sidelong glance, looked into the rear view mirror, and pulled away from the curb. After what seemed an endless silence I asked, "What did Mom have to say?"

"She wants to see you and the boys, but I told her I'm not ready to send you up there anytime soon."

With everything that was happening, I thought visiting Mom wasn't such a bad idea. I didn't even hate her right then. Too much had happened, I didn't know what to think or feel about anything.

"So, what do you have to say for yourself?" asked Dad.

"You're really upset with me, aren't you?"

"Well, can you blame me? Leaving your brothers alone like you did is unthinkable. I should have grounded you for skipping school before I left. Though at this point, I don't even know if you'd have obeyed me."

I looked straight ahead and answered. "I'm sorry. And I told the boys I'm sorry." I sensed Dad's eyes turning toward me. He veered to the right lane, instead of the left which would have taken us home.

"Where are you going?"

"Martin's Dairy. We need to talk. Officer Murgio, who brought you home Friday night, called this afternoon."

My heart stabbed at my chest.

"He says the Weavers are bringing charges of vandalism."

"No! We didn't wreck his boat!"

"I told him I didn't believe you would do anything like that. But I don't know about your companion."

"His name is Caleb," I croaked through tears, "and he's my best friend. At least he was."

"Okay. Murgio says you and Caleb were plainly sober. He wants to get all the facts. He doesn't know what you were doing at the—"

"I tried to explain to him, and he wouldn't listen." I sniffed. "We were looking for Caleb's brother."

"Right. Well that's beside the point now. Those charges of the Weavers are serious. But the other thing is, Murgio wants to know how all the alcohol and drugs got there in the first place. The Weaver kid claims the party was crashed by guys he didn't know and they brought the drinks.

"Yeah right."

"So you knew there was going to be alcohol there?"

"I just heard the rumors."

"Underage drinking, minors at the party, that's serious. If the Weaver kid is lying, he'll be in big time trouble himself."

"Good," I said.

"But that isn't all. Murgio's personal advice is you should stay away from your friend Caleb for a while."

I felt like I couldn't sink any lower. "What happened to Caleb on Friday night?" I asked. "He hasn't been in school, and he hasn't called me."

"He was taken home and turned over to his father." Dad turned into the Martin's Dairy drive-in lane and bought a coke for himself and a chocolate shake for me. Then he drove to the edge of the parking lot and parked under a tree.

"Another thing I asked Murgio," Dad said "was if it wouldn't be a good idea for me to go down and try to talk to the Weavers, but he doesn't advise it— says it would be better for us to find a lawyer."

"A lawyer?" My head was spinning. I could hardly take in all that he was saying.

"Missy, you're learning a hard lesson. And something else— look at me, please— I think you owe your grandparents an apology."

I got a jolt and looked him in the eyes. "No! Not Pop Pop. He should be the one apologizing to me after the way he talked about Caleb and me. He called him a coon. And he called me a 'tramp'."

Dad shifted in his seat and sighed. "He shouldn't have done that. But you have to understand, he grew up in a different time. Right or wrong, he had a different way of looking at things. But he and Nana both have your best interests at heart."

I sipped on the straw and concentrated on the taste of my milkshake. A bull ant crawled across the windshield. *Do ants have racist feelings toward other ants, or is that something reserved for humans?*

"Alright, now, Missy. Tell me from the beginning," said Dad. "Tell me about you and this Caleb and exactly what you were up to on Friday night."

"I told you already why we went there. And I didn't expect to be there more than a minute. You know, I thought we'd just go to the door and ask for Joshua."

"Did you know there was no supervision at the party?" Dad asked.

"Well, yeah. Everyone knew that."

Dad shook his head as he took a sip of soda.

"Mostly, I just wanted to see inside the Weaver's house."

"Tell me about Caleb," said Dad. "Even I have a hard time with you saying this black boy is your best friend."

"See. That's the problem. The thing is, I didn't have any friends here. Hardly anyone was nice to me until he became my friend. After that, things were different. Almost everyone likes him."

Dad looked at me for a long moment. "I didn't realize this move was so hard for you, Missy. But tell me, why did the two of you skip school and go off together on the bus last week? That doesn't look good."

"We went to Asher Park to work on our science project."

"Asher Park. It's pretty isolated up there on week days."

"Dad! What are you saying?" I raised my voice. "He and I are friends. His dad is a minister, and Caleb is . . . like spiritual!"

Dad held up his hand. "Okay. You don't need to shout. I wasn't really implying anything. Just that you shouldn't have been up there. That's all."

"We needed to get good material for our project. And Caleb is totally involved with his drawings. When we were in the woods we were both drawing, and he drew a deer that walked right up beside us. You should see his drawings, Dad. They're awesome!"

"And I would like to see his drawings." Dad looked at his watch. "I think we'd better get back or Pop Pop will start to worry, and we don't want that."

Dad drove along quietly for a while. Then he said "This could be a long ordeal. I just hope you'll start talking to Nana and Pop Pop again."

"With Pop Pop that's going to be hard," I said.

"A lot of things are hard, including my having to tell you you're restricted to the house when you're not in school, until this thing is resolved. No going out. No talking on the phone."

"Okay," I said.

It probably didn't matter anyhow. Where was I going to go? It's not like I was popular or anything. Latanya was a cheerleader, so she was always busy, and Caleb— well even if I were allowed to see him— I felt myself sinking into a funk and wondered if I'd ever get out.

CHAPTER 19

Accusations

The week had crept by, with me worrying about how Caleb would act toward me when I next saw him. Would he even speak to me. Wednesday was the first day that Caleb and Joshua were back in school. When I finally went up to Caleb after ecology class, I just said I was sorry about his grandma. And he said, "Thanks, Missy."

Even though I was not supposed to hang out with Caleb (which I didn't exactly tell him), I didn't think talking to him when I'd see him in class should count.

In art class Caleb actually seemed pretty much like his normal self. He showed me the cover he made for our science project, which was due in two days. Otherwise he was quiet with his face in his drawing. Of course I told him I was on restriction and not allowed to go anyplace but school, and not allowed to talk on the phone, and he said he had some restrictions of his own.

Ms. Coplan had an ear for what was happening with her students, and she was really understanding toward Caleb and me. She knew kids were talking about us and she said we could eat lunch in her room with a few other students she allowed to do that. She told us she didn't believe for one minute that we had vandalized that boat. I really liked her.

Now Joshua sauntered up to the table where Caleb, Latanya and I were sitting. "Our Daddy told Caleb not to hang with you," Joshua said to me.

"Shut up, Joshua," said Caleb.

I felt sick. Did Caleb tell his daddy about what Pop Pop said?

"It's true," said Joshua. "I don't have nothin' against you, Missy. I told him it's probably not your fault."

"You know they didn't do anything wrong," said Latanya, but Joshua walked away without saying anymore.

Maybe his daddy thought I got Caleb in trouble. Maybe he's just like Pop Pop. Or maybe Officer Murgio told him to tell Caleb to stay away from me.

When the lunch bell rang, Joshua was the first one out of the room, as usual, and Latanya, who had gotten a part in the school play, hurried off to the drama room. She was eating lunch there now so she could get in extra practice time. Everyone was out of the art room for the moment, leaving Caleb and me alone. The radio was on and playing a sad song. Caleb was not saying anything, and I dared ask a question that had been on my mind.

"What about Joshua? Where was he that night?" I unwrapped my egg salad sandwich and the smell permeated the room.

Caleb was using his kneaded eraser to make highlights in his drawing. "Joshua's not mad at you. It's me he wants to get at."

I didn't know what he was talking about. "Why should Joshua be mad at you?"

"The police came to our house yesterday," said Caleb.

"They did?"

"Yup. I thought they were coming for me, but it was Joshua they wanted to see."

"You're kidding."

"No. Someone from the party told them they saw Joshua headed for the boat. When the police came to our house, and Joshua learned they wanted to see him, he freaked."

"So, what did he tell them?" I asked.

"He said he walked out to look at the boat, then left when he heard loud noises coming from inside. Said he was getting ready to leave anyhow, because he was the only black brother at the party, and he didn't like the way some guys were looking at him."

"Do you believe him? I mean, why didn't he say that before? That might have helped us."

"I believe him. But he told them he had no idea what time it was, and since he didn't see who was down in the boat— as far as the police are concerned— it could have been us."

"It must have been a lot earlier than the time we were there," I said.

"Yup. But Joshua is pissed at me. He likes to see me get in trouble. Even though Daddy was mad as a wet hen with me for going to the party, he believed me when I said I didn't do anything."

"And did he believe Joshua?"

"Don't know," said Caleb. "Joshua lied to him about even being at the party."

"In a way your dad sounds like my Pop Pop," I said. "You know . . . I'm sorry about the way my Pop Pop acted on Friday night. I've stopped going over there and I' m not speaking to him."

Caleb looked at me. "Better speak to him. He won't be around forever."

There was an awkward silence, and then Caleb took out a bag of cookies from his backpack.

"Hey, are you supposed to be eating that stuff?" I blurted out.

He looked at me surprised.

"I know you have diabetes," I said. "Here. I have half a sandwich left. It's on whole wheat bread and it's got lots of protein."

"Don't worry about it," said Caleb. "I'm alright."

Ms. Coplan came into the room and sat at her seat with a salad and drink. Other students came in, and Caleb ate his cookies. He didn't say anymore.

* * *

I was in Dad's room at his computer typing in an on-line search. "*D-I-a-b-e-t-e-s, l-I-f-e- -e-x-p-e-c-t-a-n-c-y.*"

I heard someone coming up the stairs, and by the sound of the footsteps, I knew it must be Nana, and I closed out the site.

"Online?" she said. "I hear that can be habit forming."

"Hi, Nana. Just working on my science project."

"Oh that's good. When's it due?"

"Friday," I said.

She pulled up a chair beside me and I started another search. *F-l-o-r-i-d-a-- a-l-l-i-g-a-t-o-r.*

"I was just wondering how you're doing," she said. "I worry about you."

"Yeah, well I'm not doing much of anything for a while."

"I know," said Nana. "I just want to be sure you know I believe what you said. I know you couldn't do what they're accusing you of."

"Thanks, Nana, but what about Pop Pop?" I turned to see her face when she answered.

"Your Pop Pop certainly doesn't believe you are responsible for that vandalism. But you know how he is. Once he gets upset, it's hard to get him over it."

"You mean about leaving the boys alone?"

"Yes. And going off with that black boy. I can't understand that either, Missy."

I turned back to the computer and stared at the sites I had brought up. "Florida alligator," "alligator endangered," and "alligator hunting."

After a while Nana got up. "Well, I guess I'll get on back. She left without my saying good-bye.

C H A P T E R   2 0

The Thing with Amber

Friday finally arrived. The whole town of Turtle River was really into the high school's football games, and I heard there had been a crowd at Thursday afternoon's homecoming parade. Our middle school band marched in the parade and tonight they were going to play along with the high school band in the half time show at the game. Most kids had their minds on those events instead of what happened the past weekend. That was good with me. I, of course, being restricted, couldn't go to any of it. Didn't matter. I was tired after staying up late the night before to finish the science project. I really went over and beyond and so did Caleb.

I had fifteen descriptions of animals that lived in the park, and Caleb had drawings to go with each description. We gave our presentation in Mr. R's class first thing that morning, and we passed Caleb's drawings around so everyone could see them close up. The class was blown away by them. We hadn't gotten our grades yet, but I could tell Mr. R. was impressed with all of it. I even included the legends of the owls. Why not? Caleb had drawings that fit with those stories, too.

In art class Latanya, Caleb, and I were sitting together, working on our paintings that were due the next week. Joshua was sitting at the next table and was begging a girl beside him for a lick from her lollypop. And she actually let him have it, even though, I could tell, she didn't want to.

Amber came in wearing dark glasses. She handed Ms. Coplan a note, came to our table and sat next to Caleb across from Latanya and me. She had been out the past couple of days.

"Girl, what's goin' on with you?" Latanya asked her.

"Nothing," Amber said.

"I know there's something," said Latanya. "And it probably has to do with that boyfriend of yours."

"I broke up with him this morning," said Amber.

Amber spoke softly. I stared at my paper and strained my ears to hear. I saw Caleb slowly dip his brush in water.

"Well, finally you did something smart," said Latanya.

"They kicked me out of cheering," said Amber. She started to cry, and put her head down on the table.

"I told you that would happen if you missed all those practices," said Latanya. Then she went back to her painting, as if she'd forgotten Amber.

I watched Caleb and saw him give Amber a sympathetic look.

Amber took off her glasses, found a tissue in her purse, wiped her eyes, and blew her nose. Everyone was looking at her, including Ms. Coplan, who started to head our way, then changed her mind.

Even I felt sorry for Amber. It seemed like Latanya was being a little chilly to her, but then I knew she'd really tried to talk sense to her in the past.

When the bell rang Caleb and I followed Amber and Latanya out of the room. Caleb hadn't said much to me, and I knew he was annoyed with me for telling him what he should and should not be eating yesterday. But then he asked me if I wanted to eat in the cafeteria instead of with Ms. Coplan, since he didn't bring his lunch and would be buying it. Restriction or not I told him yes.

When I stepped out the door I saw Doyle standing in the hallway. I immediately felt a sense of dread.

"Amber, I've got to talk to you," he said and took her by the arm. She moved away and he jerked her back. "Come on Amber."

"Hey! Doyle," Caleb shouted. "Why don't you leave her alone? She doesn't want to be around you."

Doyle turned to Caleb, and sneered. "What are you talking about, boy? Aren't you in trouble enough?" He pushed Caleb.

I couldn't believe what was happening. Caleb recovered and pushed Doyle back. In an instant, Doyle was at Caleb, grabbing him by the neck and slamming him against a locker. I was yelling, "Stop!" Amber was screaming, and kids were circling around us when Mr. Creek, the art teacher from across the hall, grabbed Doyle from behind. Mr. Creek was a huge man and no one was going to mess with him.

"You two come with me," he said. Caleb was on the floor. Ms Coplan and one of the guys from our class tried to help him up, but he brushed them off and got himself up. Mr. Creek waited for him and then escorted both boys to the office.

"Who saw how that started?" asked Ms. Coplan.

"I did," I said immediately.

"Not you Missy. Somebody else."

I felt bad Ms. Coplan didn't let me go, but I guess with the trouble I was in with Caleb, I wasn't a good choice.

Anyhow Latanya and a boy from class volunteered, Ms. Coplan told them to come with her so she could write a note for them to go to the office and report what they saw.

What was Caleb thinking? Why should he be so concerned about Amber? And now what kind of trouble was he going to be in?

CHAPTER 21

The Game

I was lying on my bed with Sam, glad it was Friday afternoon, but feeling depressed about everything that was going on, when Dad opened the door and stood in the doorway.

Sheez. Couldn't he knock? I could be in here naked.

"How about we all go to the football game tonight?" Dad asked cheerfully.

"I thought I was restricted," I said.

"You're restricted only from going out on your own or with friends, not with us."

"What friends?" I was doubtful about Caleb's friendship now, and why would I want to go to the stupid football game?

Dad ignored my comment. "One of the teachers at the college had tickets for four reserved seats he couldn't use, so he gave them to me."

"I think I just want to stay here."

"Come on Missy. You've been lying around in your room all week. I want you to come out with us. You're not ashamed to be seen with your old man and your little brothers, are you?"

"Yeah Missy," said Ryan who appeared from behind Dad.

"I don't want to go."

Ryan crossed the room and climbed onto the bed with me and grabbed me around the neck. "You have to go."

"Unfair. This is like a conspiracy," I said.

I could never say no to Ryan. I didn't think he would ever be one to hold a grudge. His eye was looking better and the swelling on his forehead had gone down. He put his hands on my shoulders and put his face up to mine, nose to nose. "You gotta go."

"Okay. Okay. I'll go," I said, pulling him away from me. "But don't expect me to have fun."

Ryan bounced up and down on the bed. "She's going. Yay! Yay!"

* * *

Right after we got to the athletic field, we walked along the fence while drums were rolling as the marching bands were filing to the bleachers. I watched a familiar looking girl with a flute march past me and realized it was Beth. I never knew she was in the band. She was a nice girl, and I felt ashamed that I once thought I was too good for her. She'd been doing a lot better than I was.

I followed Ryan and Richie, who followed Dad to our seats in front of the fifty yard line. I wondered if Caleb might be there or if the trouble he got into that afternoon had caused him to be restricted even more.

"Missy!"

I turned and saw Latanya waving from the other side of the fence where the middle school cheerleaders were joining the high school cheerleaders.

"Are you off restriction?" she called as she ran up to me.

"No, I'm here with my dad and brothers. What happened with Caleb and Doyle this afternoon? Is Caleb okay?"

"He's okay. I don't think he got in trouble after we reported what happened. I don't know what they did about Doyle, though."

"I hope he gets suspended," I said.

"I never saw Caleb get in a fight with anyone. That was weird," said Latanya.

I heard Ryan calling me through the crowd. The football players were coming out on the field. I told Latanya I'd talk to her later and we separated.

I joined Dad and the boys in the stands. We were just high enough for me to see the people arrive and to see who was milling around down below, but I couldn't see everyone who was in the student section. I saw Joshua walk by with friends, but Caleb wasn't among them. I thought of calling him earlier—despite the restriction—but then I thought his dad might answer and he might think of me like Pop Pop thinks of Caleb. Now I wondered, why did Caleb care about Amber so much that he would get into a fight over her?

The players came to the side of the field. After we stood for the national anthem, I noticed Ms. Coplan several rows beneath us in the teacher section. Now the bands marched onto the field for the pre-game show. I looked at the cheerleaders lined up in their blue and gold uniforms. The middle school cheerleaders were in red skirts with white tops, our school colors. But tonight they were wearing blue and gold ribbons for the high school. Latanya was the only black girl out there. There were not many blacks at our schools, but I thought that there should be more than one black cheerleader.

Ryan and Richie sat between me and Dad. "Can I have popcorn, Dad?" Richie asked.

Dad dug into his pocket, pulled out a ten, and handed it to me. "Here Missy, go on down to the stand with Richie and get something for the boys and yourself."

"I want to go, too!" called Ryan.

"No, you stay here," Dad said.

Ryan started to cry, "It isn't fair. Richie gets to do everything."

Dad rolled his eyes and gave in. I glared at him. "Are you sure you trust me with both of them?"

"I trust you can take care of them," he said, looking me firmly in the eyes. "There aren't so many people walking around down there now. Just hold Ryan's hand."

"You boys stay right with your sister," he added.

I felt self-conscious walking along in front of the bleachers, but the bands' show had begun, and hopefully everyone was watching that. Still, I saw kids from school milling around. One girl from art class said "Hi", and right after that a little boy walking with his dad said "hi" to Ryan. Ryan smiled.

"Who was that?" I asked.

"Carlos, from school," he said, and broke from my hand to run ahead with Richie to the refreshment stand. There was no line and few people standing around, so I didn't make a big deal of his running ahead. I just took their orders when I got there—a box of popcorn for each of them and an extra-large soda for me, which I'd be sharing when they decided they were thirsty.

I got the boys to carry their popcorn and hung onto Ryan with one hand and the soda with the other. When we were back in the stands I saw Joshua again walking with his friends, but I never did see Caleb. The bands had left the field, and the football players had come back. The cheerleaders demonstrated what they do best, and I watched Latanya do a series of flips. She was definitely the best one out there, even better than the high school cheerleaders in my opinion.

Touchdown! Everyone screamed and jumped up and down. The drums rolled and the horns bellowed. Then I sat back down again and felt something cold and wet on my seat. Ryan had spilled the soda.

I never did like football and wished this game would hurry up and get over with.

CHAPTER 22

A Turn of Events

It was a short week at school. Monday had been a holiday and Friday was going to be a teachers' planning day. And today was already Thursday. We had done our end of the six week marking period tests in all our classes that week, and I'd been spending a lot of time studying, since my grades in some of my subjects had not been so great. Mr. R. let Caleb and me know we had an A+ on our science project. Caleb did not get into trouble because of the fight. Ms. Coplan saw to that. She went to the office as soon as she could and talked to the principal. Doyle, on the other hand, was suspended for a week. Hooray!

I came into the art room and saw Caleb at his regular seat and Amber sitting next to him. That was okay. There were no real assigned seats, but did she have to have her chair pulled so close to his? All week she'd been hanging on him. She was so pathetic.

I guessed I did have to give Amber credit for having a few brains, since she did break up with Doyle. Not that I really cared. Yesterday she had her head down on the table so her long red hair spread out all around, even touching Caleb's drawing. I felt like grabbing the whole wad of it and pulling her out of the seat. Caleb just picked up the strands on his drawing and moved them so he could draw. Later on, when we were waiting for the bell to ring, I saw her hug him.

As for Doyle, I was finding out that a lot of kids didn't like him and were even saying they knew he was the one who put the swastika on Mr. R.'s door. And it had become common knowledge he was a racist.

"Missy," called Ms. Coplan, as I got my drawing materials from my drawer. "Could you come over to my desk for a moment?"

That made my nerves prick up. What could she have wanted to talk to me about? At least she was smiling.

"Were those your brothers at the football game?"

"Yes"

"Cute boys." she said. "I was really impressed with how attentive you were with them. I was wondering, would you be interested in baby-sitting for me? I have a three-year-old daughter, and my usual sitter isn't available."

"Sure, I'd like that," I said. "I have to ask my dad."

"This is for Saturday afternoon. If you're busy, that's okay."

"No, I'm not busy, but I'm...still not allowed to go out on my own. Maybe you could bring her to my house. She could play with my brothers. That is if it's convenient for you."

Ms. Coplan's freckled face lit up. "That would work, and I'm sure she would love to play with your brothers. You ask your dad, and I'll get back with you."

I sat down by Latanya across from Caleb. Latanya gave me a questioning look, and I told her what Ms. Coplan wanted. Caleb looked up from a new drawing he'd been working on and smiled at me.

Joshua popped in the door. "Joshua, you're late again," called Ms. Coplan. "And don't give me that stuff about the shop teacher. I'm onto that. It's detention time. You can't keep doing this and not expect consequences."

Joshua mumbled something and pulled up a chair next to Amber who had on headphones and was actually working for a change. Ms. Coplan handed Joshua a detention slip. I think she had given up on him. He never worked.

My mood changed again, and I started feeling philosophical and a little depressed. Now that we were through with our science project, I realized there was no reason for me to talk with Caleb like before. He was there to be my friend when I needed him, and now I guessed he was there for Amber. Maybe he liked charity cases. But there was more to it than that with us— he told me things he had never told anyone else. But, he never did talk about his diabetes. Now he either had his nose in his drawings, or he was staring out into space. I didn't know if he was seeing or talking to Amber outside of school. Of course, Caleb and I still had the question of the boat trashing hanging over our heads, as did Joshua it seemed. How miserable could I be?

CHAPTER 23

When Nellie Came

Dad gave his okay for me to babysit, though he hadn't met Ms. Coplan yet.

At just a little after noon on Saturday Sam barked and bounded to the front door. When I opened it he was all over Ms. Coplan and her daughter, Nellie. Luckily they were dog people, and after the initial ruckus Ms. Coplan bent down and gave Nellie a kiss— right after Sam licked Nellie on the face. Ms. Coplan told us good-bye and then was gone. Nellie was really a cute little kid, with long brown curls pulled back into a pony tail and big brown eyes. With a pink suitcase in hand she marched down the hall and into the great room, as if she had done that a million times before, and she opened the suitcase spilling a dozen Barbie dolls onto the floor. She insisted I play with her. I remembered my Barbie days from when I was little, although I never had as many as Nellie. These were mostly naked with their long hair in a tangled mess. There were clothes in the suitcase and Nellie tried unsuccessfully to dress one doll. She wouldn't let me help, but told me which was my doll and what clothes I was to put on her. She soon tired of that and wandered around the house stopping at the stairs. I let her go up following behind her and made sure Dad's bedroom door was closed. It was a mess up there, and even though she was only three, I really didn't want her to see it. Besides there were a lot of things she could get into. She said she didn't have stairs in her house, and then she told me her daddy didn't live with her anymore. I felt a bond with her, as we both had just one parent, and I gave her a hug.

Ryan and Richie came in the house, and Nellie and I came down the stairs so she could meet them. She took to them right away and followed them around like a puppy. They laughed at her and let her play with their toy cars and Legos. Richie had other things to do, but Ryan stayed and played with her. After lunch we painted, took a walk with Sam, and we colored. Finally Nellie settled down with a pillow on the floor in the great room, with a piece of cloth she called her "silky." I lay down beside her and we watched a kid's show until she fell asleep.

I wished Dad were there, but he had to cover a ceramics workshop for a friend. I hoped he'd be home when Ms. Coplan returned. I really wanted them to meet. And I was thinking, if Nellie's daddy didn't live with them anymore, did that mean Ms. Coplan was single and alone? I hoped so.

At 5:15 pm she was not there yet and Nellie was waking up from her nap. Nana came in.

"Hi there! What's your name?" she asked, getting a sleepy look from the little girl. "Is your dad home yet?" Nana asked me. When I shook my head she went on. "I have a big pot of spaghetti sauce made for tonight. I hope you'll all come over when he gets here."

"I have to stay here with Nellie, or her mom won't know where we are."

"We can wait," she said. "Bring Nellie and her mom too."

Nana went back home. I was surprised she didn't come by much earlier, just to check on me. I had been avoiding going over there, and Pop Pop hadn't come over to our house.

I heard a car in the driveway. Sam beat me to the door, and when I looked out I saw Dad and Ms. Coplan pulling up at the same time.

"Mommy!" called Nellie. I grabbed hold of her arm— which really did annoy her— until the cars were stopped in the driveway. Released from my grip, she ran out the door to greet her mom.

Both Dad and Ms. Coplan were laughing when they get out of their cars. "Sorry I'm late, Missy, but the workshop went a little overtime," said Ms. Coplan. She picked up Nellie and hugged her. "What a surprise it was to meet your dad there."

"What? You two were at the same place?"

"Weird isn't it?" said Dad. He had a goofy smile.

This is unbelievable, it must be an omen, I thought. I told them about Nana's invite to dinner. Though Ms. Coplan said she should be going, Dad convinced her to stay.

During the meal I could see that Pop Pop liked her, and he didn't say anything awkward.

"I told Missy I was going to be at St. Andrew's High School this afternoon, but I didn't tell her it was for an art workshop." Ms. Coplan laughed.

"And I," said Dad, "told her I was teaching a workshop in ceramics, but I never said where. Lois came up to me and introduced herself, after she found out who I was. My name wasn't on the program, since I was filling in for somebody else."

"That is such a coincidence," said Nana.

"There are no coincidences," I heard myself say, followed by an embarrassing silence.

"Is that one of your ceramic pieces?" asked Ms. Coplan, pointing to the corner of Nana's living room. "It's beautiful!"

Dad nodded and thanked her.

"You ought to take her over to your studio and show her the rest," said Nana.

"Do you have time?" Dad asked.

"Sure, after Nellie's long nap, I don't think she's going to bed any time soon."

I helped Nana clear the table and Ms. Coplan took Nellie by the hand and followed Dad out of Nana's house and to our garage, which served as Dad's studio.

"She's a nice lady," said Pop Pop. "Much better than those other ones your Dad came home with." I didn't say a word.

In the kitchen, Nana took me aside." Aren't you ever going to speak to your Pop Pop again?"

"Not unless he says he's sorry for the way he talked about my friend."

"You and Pop Pop. You're just alike," Nana said and shook her head. "Go on over to your house and help watch the boys and Nellie while your dad shows Lois around."

"Okay. Thanks, Nana, for dinner." And I left without giving Pop Pop a passing glance. My mind moved forward. *What could be more cool than Dad and Ms. Coplan getting to know each other?*

I looked up at the sky and saw billions of stars shining down on us. Nellie and Ryan and Richie were running around in the front yard, chasing Sam, screaming and laughing together. *This is good.*

"Is there a court date?" I heard Ms. Coplan ask when I came up behind her.

Dad nodded toward me, and she turned around. "No," he said. "They're still examining the evidence and there hasn't been enough to press charges. But Missy and Caleb are still suspects."

"Well," she said, looking at me. "I wish they'd get this mess cleared up. I have confidence in Missy and Caleb. They didn't do it.'

Dad smiled. "Missy seems to think a lot of that boy, Caleb."

"He's a good kid," Miss Coplan said, "but he's had some hard knocks to deal with, and he's overcome them. His dad came by in the first week of school and visited all of his teachers. He really doesn't have to worry about Caleb. I've never seen anyone work so hard. He's a natural at drawing, and I think he'd do well in ceramics, too. Unfortunately, the ceramics teacher we have is a real slug."

Dad laughed. "I told Missy I'd like to see Caleb's work. Maybe I can help him get started in ceramics."

"That would be wonderful," said Ms. Coplan. "What I'd really like is to see him get accepted into the School of the Arts. That way he'd have a better chance for a scholarship later, which he would need. His father is well thought of in the community, but he doesn't have much financially." Ms. Coplan brightened. "Say, you can see his work if you come to the school next Saturday for our Fall Festival. There's an art show, band concert and all kinds of other things going on. You have to come and stop by the art room. Missy's work will be on display in our gallery. She has some good work too."

I wasn't sure if she really meant that last part or just thought she had to say it. But Dad agreed to go, and said he would forget about the restriction one more time. My dad and my favorite teacher! If that wasn't cool. *Now if I only could get my best friend back.*

CHAPTER 24

The Fall Festival

"When are we going to get ice cream?" asked Richie.

"After we see Missy's art work," said Dad.

I led Dad, the boys, and Nana through the crowd toward the fine arts building. Pop Pop wasn't feeling well and didn't want to come, but I thought that was an excuse and he just didn't want to come anyhow. I was still keeping my distance from him, but even the boys had been complaining about his grouchiness. I was just glad he wasn't there with us. Besides he never liked crowds, and this was definitely a crowd.

Earlier we sat and ate barbecued chicken on the patio while the band played under a large tent on the grass. There I met Latanya with her parents. Her mother was pretty just like Latanya, and her dad, who owns a hardware store, was also nice looking. We went through all the introduction stuff before she left to get ready for her performance in the play.

The festival was a lot bigger thing than I thought it would be. There were vendors along the walkway— a lot of them dressed in costumes, since the next Tuesday was Halloween.

Dad pushed me from behind, and we went into the gallery of the fine arts building, which separated the visual arts side of the building from the music side.

Caleb told me he wouldn't be there because he was busy with something else. It seemed he was always busy with something else lately. And he was even quieter than usual in art class all last week.

Amber hadn't been hanging around him as much as she had been, and I supposed it was true his dad told him to stay away from me.

Dad, Nana, and the boys wandered around looking at the work on the walls.

"I saw Missy's drawing!" shouted Ryan. Dad stopped at one of Caleb's owl drawings and inspected it closely. Nana commented on how beautiful it was and on how much talent there was at the school.

"Hi! Glad you made it." I turned at Ms. Coplan's voice and saw Caleb's dad standing beside her. "Have you ever met Brother Jones?"

Before we could answer, one of the other students interrupted to tell Ms. Coplan she was wanted on the phone. "Oh dear. Brother Jones, these are the Vicellies. Missy is a friend of Caleb's. You ought to talk to her dad; he's an art teacher at the college. Now if you'll excuse me..." Ms. Coplan waved and hurried off to her office.

Dad was shaking hands with Brother Jones. "Dave Vicelli," he said, then introduced Nana, and me— the boys were wandering around. I was really glad Pop Pop wasn't here. Brother Jones looked soberly at me and said in a soft voice that we had already met.

"Your son is very talented," said Dad. "My area is ceramics. I'd like to see what he could do with that."

"Yes. Caleb is a fine artist. He's been drawing for as long as he's been able to hold a crayon."

Then there was an awkward silence and Dad said, "I guess you and I should sit down and talk sometime about this situation our two children are involved in. There hasn't been a date for them to go to court yet, and hopefully it will be cleared up before that is necessary."

Brother Jones shook his head. "We try to raise them up right and sometimes we succeed." He stared at Dad, and then spoke slowly and directly. "I believe my son when he says he didn't do anything wrong. There is another matter of which I'd like to speak to you."

I felt like my heart had stopped. What was he going to say?

"We're having a celebration at our church Monday night," Brother Jones said looking at Dad. "Caleb would like your daughter to come, but he was too embarrassed to ask her. I'd like to invite all of you. There's going to be a surprise."

"Well, thank you," said Dad, looking a little bewildered. "Yes, we'll try to make it."

"Very well." Brother Jones nodded. "Ms. Coplan said she would come also." He smiled slightly, then looked at his watch. "I've got to be going. I have a funeral I must officiate. Nice meeting you folks." After that Brother Jones was out the door.

Unbelievable. Why would Caleb be embarrassed to ask me to this celebration at his church? Dad and Nana looked at each other curiously.

"He didn't say what time," said Dad. "Missy, you'll have to ask Caleb what time."

I just nodded and smiled as we left, trying to figure out why it was important for me to come to his church. More people were coming into the gallery and Ms. Coplan was still not back, so Dad said we might as well head on out to the ice cream stand.

On the way there I saw Amber walking along ahead of us, holding hands with a boy. Not Doyle, but an older looking boy I didn't recognize. What a difference a day made. In the back of my mind I wondered if she was invited to the ceremony at the church. Then I felt certain that she wasn't.

CHAPTER 25

Hallelujah! Amen

Ms. Coplan pulled into the parking spot next to us in her red Wrangler. We were among the first to arrive. When we got out of the car a middle aged black lady in a pink dress and a big pink hat rushed over to us. "Hi there, I'm Ayida. Why don't ya'll come on in."

We introduced ourselves and followed Ayida through the church's double doors into a small entry way. Another lady hugged us like we were long lost friends, gave us each a program, and led us down a creaky wooden floor of the near vacant sanctuary to the third row of seats. I went in first, Ms. Coplan followed and then Dad.

"This is lovely," said Ms. Coplan. "Look at those chandeliers. They give the room a beautiful golden glow."

I looked around. Compared to the churches I'd been in, this was very small. In the front, the pulpit— from where the minister speaks— was on a small stage with an altar at the back against a curtain that had a cross painted on it. On the stage to the left were a set of drums and two chairs.

It wasn't long before the vacant seats in the sanctuary began to fill and the quiet chamber began to hum. I heard Dad say a little too loudly to Ms. Coplan, "I feel like a slob." He voiced my feelings, exactly. He, in his khaki pants and polo shirt, and me in my denim dress— the only dress I owned. Ms. Coplan did a little better in a long skirt and silk blouse. The men of the church were dressed in suits, and the ladies looked like they were going to a wedding—in an array of color and fancy hats.

A lady and a little boy, about two-years-old, sat in front of us next to an old lady with a small, navy blue straw hat on her head. The little boy stood on the seat and looked back at us with impish black eyes.

"Hi Tiger. What's your name?" asked Ms. Coplan.

"Micah." He giggled and hid his face. His mother turned and smiled at us, then sat Micah back on the seat.

"You should have brought Nellie," I whispered to Ms. Coplan.

To that she laughed and rolled her eyes. "She'd be all over the place," she said. Then Dad started to talk to Ms. Coplan from the other side, leaving me with my thoughts.

I remembered when we lived in Pennsylvania, we used to go to Sunday school and church regularly. Mom was really into religion then. She was at Bible studies once a week, before she got into theater. But it was at a Bible study that she met the guy she ran off with. That was the end of church for me, Dad, and the boys. Dad only went to please Mom, anyhow. Since we moved to Turtle River, Nana did try to get us back to church, but with no success— not even with Ryan and Richie. Nana would have come to this event, but she stayed home with the boys and Pop Pop, who was still not feeling well.

Caleb walked by us and took a seat up front on the opposite side of the aisle. He turned around and flashed a smile at us. I had asked Caleb in school what this celebration was about and what the surprise was, but he wouldn't even give me a hint. Latanya was in the dark about it, too, and Joshua acted like he didn't care.

Latanya came into our row and sat by me, just as Brother Jones came down the center aisle, shaking hands with people on his way. He stopped by us. "Glad to see you folks this evening."

"Thank you. It's nice to be here," said Ms. Coplan, and Dad agreed. I just wondered what Brother Jones really thought of all of us— especially me.

Latanya poked me and pointed to the stage. I saw Joshua come up and sit behind the drums. Another boy came up with a trumpet and sat in the chair beside Joshua.

"I didn't know he played the drums," Ms. Coplan whispered. Neither did I.

Reverend Jones went onto the stage and sat next to the pulpit. Two men and three women rose from the front row and stood in front of the stage facing the congregation. One man adjusted the microphone and they begin to sing with rhythm, waving their hands and clapping.

"My Lord is calling me,
Oh my Lord is calling me.
I hear the trumpet call,
I hear the trumpet call."

The singers repeated the lyrics, and then added:

"I hear the thunder roll,
I hear the thunder roll.
My L-o-r-d is calling me home."

Joshua rolled his drums, and the trumpeter bellowed out. Then the choir repeated the song.

A man began to play an organ, located at the right side of the stage, and the people in the congregation stood and sang along and clapped with the choir. Then the words changed and the congregation chanted "P-r-a-i-s-e Lord Jesus! P-r-a-i-s-e Lord Jesus!" Everyone swayed and waved their hands in the air. The tempo picked up, and soon they were clapping again and singing, "Praise Jesus, Praise," over and over. The old lady in front of us moved away from her seat and danced in the aisle waving a tambourine.

Latanya was swaying and moving her hands and chanting, and I could see Caleb on the other side of the aisle doing the same. Ms. Coplan and Dad had joined in, and I, too, began to clap and wave my hands, timidly at first, but soon I forgot myself and was caught up in the fever and fell into the spirit with everyone else. With the organ and the chanting and the instruments, it was thunderous and ear shattering, yet I felt like we were in this little world of vibes and color and everything outside was insignificant. Then the music stopped. The choir returned to their seats, and everyone else sat down.

This was a Methodist church, but it was totally different than my old Methodist church in Pennsylvania.

Brother Jones was in the front with his hands held high. "Thank you choir. Praise Jesus. I can feel the Holy Spirit here with us tonight!"

"Oh, yes!" and "Amen" were repeated around the congregation.

"This is a special night," Brother Jones went on. "And for this special night we have special guests." *Does he mean us?* I thought.

"*My* daughters Angelina and Desiree have come to be with us." The two women Caleb was sitting with stood up and waved. Caleb's sisters. "Take time now to greet one another and tell one another of your love."

The organ music began again, and people hugged and moved into the aisles—some danced— to greet each other. Latanya gave me a hug, "I love you," she said, and then moved past me to hug Ms. Coplan. The lady in the pink hat hugged us all. Latanya moved around greeting others. She had on the long, flowing purple dress she wore in the play, where she played a flirtatious girl who was abducted by an alien.

The lady with the little boy greeted us. Caleb came into our row and gave me a hug, which gave me a warm feeling all over. Then he hugged Ms. Coplan. I introduced him to Dad and they shook hands. I felt like everything was going to be just fine. Caleb's dad welcomed us to his church and Ms. Coplan was there sitting with Dad and me. Which was a little weird but I liked it.

The choir returned to the front and began to sing again, and people went back to their seats— except for the old lady with the tambourine. She moved to the front of the choir, banging her tambourine and dancing. Joshua rolled the drums, the organ music swelled out and everyone was up and singing again. When the music finally stopped, Brother Jones raised his hands in the air and closed his eyes. He prayed for individual members of the church, and for the church to be strong for the cause of the Lord. He began softly at first, and then like the music, his tempo increased and he got louder. People in the congregation shouted out, "Praise Jesus, praise Jesus!"

After Brother Jones said, "Amen," a table was rolled to the front of the church. A basket was placed on the table, and to music from the organ, people began to move and dance to the front. Dad dug into his pocket and slipped me a bill. We all moved in the procession and dropped our money in the basket. And a man and a woman sitting at the table counted what came in.

When we were seated again, I saw a girl I recognized. It was the girl who pushed me down that day at school. She went back to her seat, right behind another girl and boy I'd seen around school. *What will she think of me now? Here at her church.*

After everyone returned to their seats, Brother Jones walked to the middle of the stage with his Bible opened. As he read, the congregation followed along with their own Bibles. Brother Jones voice went up and down, hesitating at times and getting "amens" and "oh yeses" from the congregation.

Brother Jones walked back and forth while he read. He looked at the congregation. "Have you seen? My brothers and sisters, have you seen the light? Has the Holy Spirit come to you and shown you the light? I am telling you now. Don't go blabber-mouthing to everyone about your spiritual experiences. Don't tell others about it, unless. . . unless others can see by your actions what the light has done for your soul. When your goodness is seen by others, they will know you have the Spirit in your heart."

There was a chorus of "amens". Brother Jones suddenly spoke louder and faster.

I was trying to follow what he was saying. But it all sounded so strange. I remembered some of the lessons I'd learned from Sunday school and sitting through church services when I was younger, but Brother Jones way of talking was so different. And just what was this surprise we came to see? I was getting anxious to know. And I wondered what Dad was thinking about all of this? The little boy in front of me kept climbing around in his seat and looking back at us. I saw the old lady's head slowly sink to her chin, and then suddenly it bounced up again. I sometimes felt Brother Jones was looking right at me, speaking directly to me.

Joshua was looking around like he was bored. The sermon was long and everyone shouted out "yes" or "amen" when Brother Jones went over certain points.

". . . BROTHERS AND SISTERS, WILL YOU BE ON THE RIGHT SIDE OF JESUS ON JUDGEMENT DAY?"

What's Judgment Day? I thought it must be when it's decided whether or not we make it into Heaven, or if we go to that other place. Dad didn't believe in any of that. I hoped there is a heaven though, and hoped I and my family would get to see each other after we die.

". . . But when we accept Him as our Savior, we are one in him." Brother Jones was speaking very quietly now. "There is someone here who has seen the Spirit and has chosen to show what he has seen to us. He has given us a gift."

Brother Jones silently looked out into the congregation before he went on. "This someone is my own son, Caleb. He has been in this church secretly, many days and nights in the past two months. And now I want to show you what he has given to us."

What gift. What has Caleb done? I looked at Joshua and saw a confused look on his face. Brother Jones moved to the back of the stage and pulled the cord to open the large curtain against the wall. Everyone gasped when he unveiled a mural that depicted Jesus surrounded by children and animals.

Jesus was in profile, sitting on a rock at the edge of a hillside. His hair fell down over his face so his features could not be seen. But we saw the angelic faces of three little children, one white, one brown and one black, as they sat on the grass and looked up at Jesus. Behind the children, I saw the deer from Caleb's sketch book, and the squirrels were in a tree behind Jesus. There were other animals, and lying beside the children was a wolf.

I heard *hallelujahs* from the congregation and Latanya grabbed my arm. "Missy. How could he have done that without anyone knowing?" she asked.

Ms. Coplan murmured, "Caleb. My goodness. Look at what you have done."

I just sat and stared.

Brother Jones said a prayer and people began to leave their seats. I followed Latanya down the aisle toward Caleb, but he was surrounded by people, so I walked up to the mural for a closer look. On Jesus's shoulder, almost unnoticed on the white robe, sat a small white owl, its eyes looking out at me.

CHAPTER 26

Who and Why?

"Linsey, grab the masking tape," called Ms. Coplan, to one of the other eighth grade students.

Miss Coplan was dressed in black tights, a long black shirt, and dangling silver bat earrings. Today was Halloween. She was wading around in a mound of matte board, frames and pictures lying on the tables and on the floor, as we helped get work ready to send to the county art fair. It wasn't to begin until December 1st, but we had to have the work in on this day for the judging.

Caleb's painting of the owls was leaning against the wall, and four of his drawings were already matted. He was supposed to be here helping too. I hoped his English teacher would let him out of class.

"I wish we had more of his work," Ms. Coplan said, looking at me. "But I know now why he hasn't done more. I think we have enough, though, for the judges to see what he can do— and for the reps from the School of the Arts who will be there."

There were times I secretly hoped Caleb wouldn't get into the School of the Arts. After all, it would mean I wouldn't see him anymore at school. And who knew what new friends he might find.

"Come on, Missy," said Ms. Coplan. "You can put Caleb's name tags on the back of his work, and you can help me take all the work to be photographed to the patio. Paul's mom is going to bring the van around back."

Ms. Coplan handed me the name tags and the masking tape just as the jarring ring of the fire alarm caused me to jump.

"Oh no!" she yelled. "Just what we don't need!"

"I hope it's not real," somebody said.

"God forbid," said Ms. Coplan. "Come on. We have to go. It should be only a few minutes."

When we got outside in the parking lot I saw Caleb.

"Hey, are you coming to help?" I asked

"Yup. I was on my way. I had a quiz in English and my teacher wouldn't let me out until after I took it."

"I just got there myself," I said. "Coach gave me a hard time and made me run laps first."

Caleb laughed. "Hey, what you doing tonight?" he asked.

"I don't know. I'm still on restriction, but I can go to my brothers' school Halloween Carnival."

The bell rang for us to return to class, and Caleb walked beside me. "I remember that carnival, when I went to Turtle River Elementary. Maybe I could go too," he said.

My heart did a handspring. "That would be great. Why don't you come by the house, and we can go together." Then I remembered that I'm supposed to stay away from Caleb. "With my dad and the boys," I said "I think that would be okay for us to be together."

Caleb laughed. "Yeah," he said. "Next week, after we go to court, it will be all over. We know we're innocent, and I have faith, things will turn out right."

Hearing him say that made me feel that it must be true. And we could be friends again. We had both received notices the day before that we were to be at the juvenile court a week from this day— Joshua, Caleb, and I, and I didn't know who else might have been included. I just wondered what kind of evidence they found. Dad had tried to get in touch with Detective Murgio the day before, but he was out of the office and never did call back.

We entered the art room and I saw something terribly wrong.

"Oh God!" My stomach sank to my knees. Caleb's painting! The painting leaning against the wall was covered with streaks of black spray paint. I turned and glanced at Caleb standing beside me. He was frozen in place, taking quick short breaths with a look of horror on his face.

I rushed to the table where his drawings were, and what I dreaded stared me in the face. Black bands sprayed on every one of them. On the floor the work from his portfolio was spread around and in ruin.

"Oh no! No!" I heard Ms Coplan cry. I looked up and saw Caleb back away, turn and run out the door.

"Caleb!" I called. But I just stood there like a dummy watching him go.

Ms. Coplan followed after him.

What could I say to him? Tears stung my eyes and I heard the other students in the class react in shock and outrage. No other work had been touched, only Caleb's.

Ms. Coplan came back into the room with the assistant principal, who looked at the sight and shook his head. "All of your students were accounted for outside during the drill?"

"Everyone who was in the room with me was out in the parking lot," she said. "And none of them would have done this. This is so unfair! Who would want to do this to Caleb?"

I could think of one person who hated him. I hadn't seen him in a couple of days, but that didn't mean he wasn't lurking around.

The mother with the station wagon came into the room. Ms. Coplan looked at me. "Missy, you go and find Caleb and make sure he's all right. I have to finish up here and take this work down to the county office with Mrs. Osborne. I'm going to call Caleb later."

The end of the day bell had rung. I searched, and did not find Caleb. He wasn't at the bus, and neither were Joshua or Latanya. But I knew Latanya had an early orthodontist appointment. I asked some of Caleb's other friends, and they hadn't seen him or Joshua either.

I felt sick every time I thought of what happened. I was sure it was Doyle who did it. I heard someone say he heard Doyle admit he painted Mr. R's door. I was just thinking about the ways I'd like to see Doyle suffer. Staking him over a fire ant mound wouldn't be punishment enough. At the same time, I felt guilty myself for wishing that Caleb wouldn't get into the School of the Arts. It was like my secret thoughts made this happen.

CHAPTER 27

Frightening Realities

I called Caleb's house as soon as I got home, but no one answered. Later I got Joshua on the phone. He sounded really strange, and he said he didn't know where Caleb was, but he'd tell him to call me.

I was on my bed with the portable phone beside me and Sam at my feet. What could I do but lie there and wait. Dad and Nana went to the Halloween Carnival at the elementary school with the boys, and I was home, hoping the phone would ring.

Nana wanted me to check in on Pop Pop at least once, because he was still not feeling well. He had refused to go to a doctor and didn't want to be checked on by me or anyone. Even though I had been over there a few times since the night Ms. Coplan came, it wasn't the same with me and Pop Pop as it once was. I didn't think it ever would be. *If something happens to Caleb,* I thought, *though it wouldn't be Pop Pop's fault, he is just another person who has made life—*

THUMP!

What was that? Sam barked and beat me to the front door. We had the porch light on, and I had put candy on the steps in case trick-or-treaters come by. We had a few earlier, but most were probably at the carnival now.

I held Sam back, slowly opened the door, saw no one and then I looked down. My heart stopped. There was a dead sparrow at my feet. Did it fly into the door? At night? Was it an omen, or was it Doyle's doing?

I stood just outside the door, looking and listening. There, in a small oak tree next to the garage was an owl. I saw only its eyes— big eyes. I hurried into the house, shut the door and locked it. The phone rang.

I ran to my bedroom, picked up the phone with shaking hands, and sat on the edge of my bed. *Please let it be Caleb!*

"Hi Missy," it was Ms. Coplan. "Have you seen or heard from Caleb?"

I sighed. "No."

"His dad is looking for him. He's very worried."

"I've been worried too and waiting for him to call. You know it had to be Doyle who did this. He—"

"No. It wasn't Doyle."

"How do you know that? He could have snuck into the school—"

"Doyle was at the juvenile detention center at the time."

"What?"

"He and some of his friends assaulted a homeless man last night. The police came to Doyle's house and arrested him early this morning."

I was up pacing my room. "I can't believe–then. . . who?"

Ms. Coplan was silent for a moment. "It was Joshua."

"Joshua! What? Why?" I nearly tripped over Sam who was lying on the floor at the end of my bed, then I sat down.

"I know it's hard to believe. I guess it was jealousy. Caleb came home and found his mural spray painted also. Then he took off on his bike. His father knew who did it as soon as he saw it. Later Joshua broke down and admitted it to him."

"Oh no. That's horrible. That's worse than if Doyle did it."

"That it is. Plus, Brother Jones thinks Caleb hasn't had his insulin today," Ms. Coplan said. "If you hear from him at all, make sure his father knows."

"I will." We hung up, and I thought. . . *if Caleb is feeling really depressed— like I know he is— like no person on earth could help him— what would he do? Where would he go? I can only think of one place. Asher Park.*

CHAPTER 28

The Message

"No one of that description has passed through here," said the voice of the park ranger on the phone. "I've been here since two, and we've only had a couple of parties all afternoon."

I put the phone down, sank to the floor beside my bed, hugged Sam and cried. Great gushes of tears rolled down my cheeks. "God, if you're here, help me find Caleb." Suddenly Sam pulled away from me and began to bark. He ran out of the room.

BANG! BANG!

I felt blood rush through my body and followed Sam down the hallway toward the back of the house. Someone was at the door.

"Missy! Open up!"

It was Pop Pop. I rushed to the sliding door in the dining room, unlocked it, and opened it. Pop Pop nearly fell into the house. I tried to help, but he waved me off, steadied himself with one hand on his cane and the other on the dining room table.

"Are you okay?" I asked "What happened?"

"I'm okay," he said. But his face was pale, and he looked like he was going to have a heart attack. I felt a terrible dread.

"Sit down," I said pulling a chair away from the table.

"That friend of yours is in trouble," he said, ignoring me. "I saw it." What do you mean, you saw it?" I asked.

"I was sitting at my seat in the living room when I dozed off, and I dreamed. It was the clearest dream I'd ever had. It was looking at me."

"What was?"

"The messenger. The owl. It came to tell me it's my time."

I gasped, my hand went to my mouth. "Don't—don't talk like that!"

"It's your friend you need to be worried about. I saw him in my dream too, reflected in the owl's eyes. It was clear as day. The boy lying on the ground under a tree next to a lake, Pop Pop started for the door.

"Wait, Pop Pop. "Where're you going? Oh God! You mean Caleb. I know where he is! I have to get to Asher Park!"

"Come on then. Let's get in the car and find him," Pop Pop said, with a sudden burst of energy that I hadn't seen in him in a long time.

I grabbed one of the boys' thermoses from the kitchen cabinet, filled it with orange juice from the fridge, and put it in my backpack. I knew he would need some kind of sugar to keep from going into a coma and in the movies they always gave the victim orange juice. I just prayed it wasn't too late. I scribbled a note to Dad and left it on the counter.

"Let's go!" Called Pop Pop. "The car's out front."

Every stoplight seemed to turn red as we approached. The bridge over the river was raised for boat traffic, and we were forced to wait. I saw a distant lightning flash.

"I told you there was one owl," said Pop Pop. "There was a little screech owl I spotted in a tree in the woods one day. Had my sling shot with me, so I shot it down. I was a pretty good shot back then. Didn't kill it, but maimed it. Never forget that moment, when I picked it up and looked into its eyes. I felt something come over me, and I never cared much for hunting after that. That's when—"

A jagged streak flashed across the sky, followed by a loud boom. I looked at Pop Pop. He never liked thunder storms. Said they reminded him of "the War." But Pop Pop went on with his story as if the storm weren't happening at all.

"When I rescued the owlet from the bully, James LaRue, I knew I was being given a second chance. Sometimes we're given a chance to make things right. That was when I was a boy. Tonight I feel it again."

The bridge was down. Pop Pop didn't say anymore, and he drove on. I thought about the strangeness of what was happening. Here I was riding in the car with my Pop Pop, who I hadn't spoken to in weeks, and who was now making confessions from his childhood and telling me he saw Caleb in an owl's eyes in his dream.

Pop Pop turned onto the park road. The gate was locked, and the small building just inside the entrance, where the ranger was usually stationed, was dark. Pop Pop honked his horn. No one came.

"We don't have a lot of time, Missy. Take the flashlight from the glove compartment and get on in there. I'll keep the headlights on for you, and I'll keep honking."

I put the flashlight in my backpack and found myself standing in front of the fence. I was a good tree climber, though I never tried to climb a nine foot hurricane fence before. But in a couple of seconds I was up and over. Didn't even know how I did it.

The storm had ceased, the car's lights and moonlight were enough for me to find the path Caleb and I took. I looked back and waved just before moving from Pop Pops sight. Never in all my imaginings would I have thought he'd tell me to sneak into a park at night. He wasn't himself. He wouldn't have allowed me out there alone if he were.

But this was not just an adventure. This was to find and save Caleb, and now my heart was in my throat. *What if I don't find him? What if he's— oh God, don't even let me think it!* Then I remembered I didn't call Caleb's dad. I should have called him. *If only we had one of those cell phones, I could call my dad.*

I heard Pop Pop's steady honk on the horn and I made my way down the path to the lake. I kept walking and walking. After a while it seemed like I'd been walking longer than the time it should take to get there. It didn't look the same. I wasn't on the path.

A darkness closed in as the moon disappeared behind a cloud. I found my flashlight and shone it around me but I still couldn't find the path. Where was it? It was pitch black now, and I knew I was lost.

A loud crack and a flash of lightning came just before the downpour. It was pounding against the ground, like a waterfall. "Caleb! Are you out there?" My voice was overpowered by the noise of the rain. Pop Pop must have told the ranger by now and help must be on the way, I told myself.

But that was no comfort when I heard a gator grunt somewhere out there in the dark. I shivered and wrapped my arms around myself. I was soaked to the skin and I could taste my tears mixed with the rain on my lips. I heard a scream— my scream— I couldn't stop screaming and shaking. Then I whispered a small prayer. "Please God, help. Please help Caleb and me."

I didn't know how long I stood there shaking, wet and crying, when I saw a soft light just a short distance away. "Caleb? Is somebody there?" I shone my flashlight in front of me and crept toward the other light. I brushed against overhanging tree branches and within a few more steps I found myself at the edge of the lake and Caleb was there, surrounded by a golden light. He was half lying and half sitting against a tree.

My thoughts raced. He needed the juice that was in my backpack. He was shivering and seemed delirious. I fumbled around and finally got the juice out. I put it to Caleb's mouth, and though most of it spilled and ran down his chin, he did swallow a small amount. After that, I looked around and wondered what the light was that led me to Caleb. Whatever it was, it was gone now. The rain had stopped too, and in a few minutes we were sitting in moonlight. Was it just the moonlight that led me to him? No, it had been raining and dark every place but where he sat.

Caleb was not conscious of my presence, I sat next to him and put my backpack against his chest to keep the cool breeze away, and I snuggled close to help keep us both from shivering. Every once in a while I heard him moan softly, and I talked to him. I told him his owls had been watching over him, and I told him about Pop Pops vision. I sang to him.

"Amazing grace, how sweet the sound
That saved a wretch like me
I once was lost and now am found. . ."

I was drifting off when I heard a dog bark and someone called my name.

"Missy!"

"Dad?" I jumped up and saw a large German shepherd in front of me.

Within moments, Dad, a park ranger, and two other people come through the trees.

"Dad, Caleb's here," I said. "He needs help."

"Okay Baby, help is here," said Dad.

I felt tears roll down my cheeks and watched while Caleb was given a shot, covered with blankets and put on a stretcher. I was also given a blanket. A short distance away we climbed into a jeep and rode back to the park entrance. People were standing around, including Ms. Coplan and Caleb's dad. An ambulance was waiting to take Caleb to the hospital.

"Is he going to be alright?" I kept asking, but got no answers. I wanted to go in the ambulance with Caleb, but they wouldn't let me. Then, I suddenly remembered Pop Pop.

Pop Pop was right. If it weren't for him. . . I looked around. The car was there, but he wasn't. "Pop Pop! Dad, where is he?" Dad didn't say anything. He looked toward the ambulance. I tried to go to it, but Dad stopped me. I screamed. "Let me go!"

"Missy," Dad said. "It's too late. They heard the horn honking. When they got here, he was slumped over the wheel. He's gone Missy."

Dad hugged me close. "No!" I started to shake and cried hysterically. "He saw where Caleb was. He saw. . . in a vision. He saved Caleb. I didn't tell him I was sorry for not speaking to him."

"He knew that," whispered Dad.

CHAPTER 29

Afterward

Caleb stayed in the hospital for a week. The doctors said he was lucky to be found when he was. It was more than luck, I knew.

When I went to see him he didn't look like himself. He was so depressed. Not that I could blame him—seeing his work sabotaged by his brother. Ms. Coplan was at the hospital, and she told him he could do more work, even better work, but he just stared into space. It seemed he lost his will. Joshua was also there, crying, and saying he was sorry, over and over again, but Caleb wouldn't speak to him. I told Caleb I knew his owls were watching over him, and I told him about Pop Pop. Caleb didn't say anything. The doctors told us his diabetic condition was probably in part responsible for his depression.

Caleb's dad, Brother Jones, came to Pop Pop's funeral. It comforted me and I thought Pop Pop's spirit was there and that he was happy that Brother Jones came to his funeral. Brother Jones asked me to visit Caleb again. Dad took me to the hospital that day, and this time Caleb thanked me for saving him and said he only wished he could thank Pop Pop. I told him I knew Pop Pop was watching over us.

Caleb recovered quickly after that visit and was ready to go home in a couple of days. I believe Pop Pop and Caleb shared something. I believe they were both visited by angels in the form of owls. I think now that they were working with Pop Pop all his life, until finally they told him about his own passing and allowed him to save Caleb.

Eight weeks passed, and Caleb was drawing again. He fixed the mural during Christmas vacation and it looked as good as it first did.

Joshua began attending an alternative school and was receiving therapy. He really was sorry for what he did, and even though I was angry with him, I couldn't help but feel pity for him. Ms. Coplan wanted him to sign up for band and play drums when he came back to our school again. Maybe there was hope for him after all. And Ms. Coplan— she was great. She and Dad had started dating, and they were on the phone a lot. I couldn't be happier about that.

Doyle was in more trouble than his parents could get him out of, and Caleb and I were cleared from everything involved with the Weaver's boat. The police finally got a lead that led them to some so-called friends of Doyle's from his old neighborhood in another town. They were the ones who crashed the party and vandalized the boat.

Caleb was to start at the School of the Arts in the fall. Ms. Coplan did no small amount of politicking to get him in. And it didn't hurt that she had taken pictures of his work before it was vandalized. For me, his getting into the School of the Arts meant I wouldn't see him in school anymore. But Dad was giving Caleb lessons in ceramics, so for now, I saw a lot of him. And no matter what the future holds, I knew Caleb and I would be friends forever. I had new goals for myself now. I started writing down all the stories that Pop Pop told, and I began writing about the experiences I had with Caleb.

I had started a letter to Mom. I didn't know if she and I would have a relationship in the future, but after what I'd experienced in the past few weeks, I believed that anything was possible.

Author of the middle grade novella *Tales of Turtle River,* Sherry Williams has been an art teacher, substitute teacher, library media specialist and artist. Now when she isn't writing she is volunteering in church related food programs, exercising in the gym, and spending time with her grandchildren. She has belonged to a writing group for close to 30 years, and she recently formed a book club. Sherry is married to artist and former art teacher, Grant Williams. Grant is the cover illustrator for *Eyes of the Owl.* Sherry and he live in Jupiter, Florida with their two dogs. They have two sons and seven grandchildren.

Printed in the United States
By Bookmasters